Also by Carl Dane:
Hawke and Carmody Western Novels
Valley of the Lesser Evil
Canyon of the Long Shadows
Rage under the Red Sky
Blood Beneath the Hunter's Moon

Rapid Fire Reads (short books)
Delta of the Dying Souls
The Mountain of Slow Madness
Fury on the Far Horizon

ISBN: 9781707224470

BLOOD
BENEATH THE
HUNTER'S MOON

A HAWKE & CARMODY WESTERN NOVEL

CARL DANE

RAGING BULL PUBLISHING

Dedication

To Mark and Carl III.

Chapter 1

The mail, like everything else around here – except for trouble – moves slowly, which explains why I'd received a letter from a dead man asking for my protection.

It was a bizarre coincidence, but these things happen, which I suspect is why we invented the word "coincidence." I'd gotten the two-week-old letter from someone named Gus Marner the same afternoon I'd received the one-week-old newspaper that carried an article about his suicide.

The letter was dated Sept. 25, 1877, and was written in a cramped and shaky hand that slanted steeply downhill. I've heard that down-sloping writing indicates pessimism, and from the looks of things it was warranted.

To Josiah Hawke
Town Marshal, Shadow Valley, Texas

Dear Marshal Hawke:
You do not know me but I have read about you and know that you are familiar with the casino business. I am the owner of Marner's Dance and Gambling Hall in New

Paradise, Texas. It is not a large town and you may not be familiar with it, but it is within a day's ride for you, about forty miles due south of Austin and near Dead Horse and Copper Ridge.

I am facing threats here from people I do not know for reasons I do not understand. And from what gossip I have heard, mine is not the only establishment of its kind facing such harassment.

We have but the barest presence of law enforcement here, a circuit sheriff who appears infrequently.

There is much to tell you and I am not much of a writer. My point is that I will offer you 25 percent ownership of my establishment if you can provide protection. I know this is a customary arrangement in some establishments. I realize you cannot provide a constant personal presence but I am sure someone of your reputation and background can set the right people in place.

If you can meet with me I will open my books, past and present, to you. Before all this started, mine was a profitable establishment and while I do not have current resources to attract you much, I believe you will agree that if things can be set the way they were you may find yourself part of a very handsome deal.

Please return my letter or visit as quickly as you can.
Thank you.
Gus Marner

I laid the letter flat on the bar to the left of my beer and placed the folded copy of the *Dead Horse Hill Gazette* to the right. I had to squint a little because it was late afternoon and it was getting dark earlier now in early autumn and we hadn't fired up the lanterns yet because we weren't used to lighting them so early. And lately I've been having a little trouble reading the paper in dim light, which I attribute to a defect in the ink, perhaps.

ESTABLISHMENT OWNER DEAD AT OWN HAND
Gus Marner, Owner of Dance Hall and Casino, Shoots Himself Through the Head

***

Mr. Marner, a longtime resident of New Paradise, retired to his rooms above his gambling hall at about ten last night, patrons say, and was later found dead after staff investigated a gunshot heard near midnight. Apparently the man placed a pistol to his head and shot himself on the spot.

Although we do not know the cause of this sorrowful act, it has been rumored that Mr. Marner was lately of unsound mind.

Not much of an obituary, I thought, refolding the letter and dabbing it on my shirt. Even in October it can get hot in the Hill Country, and the bar top is always wet no matter how much we wipe it – wet with sweat from the sort-of-cool mugs of beer, the leftover drops of the murky gray water we use to wash the glassware, and other liquids, the origins of which I would rather not consider.

I thought about Gus Marner, wondered what could have happened in his particular world, and also wondered what I could possibly do about it now.

But it would have to wait because a second after tucking the letter into my pocket I heard angry voices, the scraping of chairs, and a gunshot.

And then my own world went to hell.

Chapter 2

The secret to being the scariest man in the room isn't necessarily size, strength, or skill with a weapon. It's usually the willingness to commit an act of violence suddenly and ruthlessly.

I was better with a gun and had a good six inches on Snake Swingle, but I was also considerably less insane than he, so I found myself at a momentary disadvantage. Swingle was holding his weapon, one of those durable old-fashioned Colt Navy single-actions favored by men who appreciated its predictable performance during regular and frequent acts of homicide, at shoulder level.

He wasn't pointing it at anyone in particular, including me, but was calmly swinging it back and forth in a metronome rhythm, covering everyone in the room, letting it be known that he would happily ventilate anyone for any reason that crossed what was left of his mind.

Across from where Swingle had been sitting was a portly fellow I didn't know who still clutched five cards in his left hand despite a neat hole in the front of his head and considerable gore exiting out the rear. His right hand hung straight down and a revolver lay on the floor a foot beneath his fingertips, which were splayed like plump sausages hanging above a butcher's counter.

As town marshal, I like to think I am accustomed to being the scariest man in the room, but with Swingle's gun intermittently pointed at me I had no immediate plan for regaining my reputation. My deputy, Tom Carmody, is generally the second-scariest, although he would tell you different, and he might be right, as he stands over six-five and is one of those rough-hewn Tennessee mountain men who is built from thick bone, sinewy gristle, and scrap iron.

Carmody was to Swingle's left, I was to the gunman's right, and Swingle was in a corner. Defensively, it was a good spot for the little man because he could cover us both, but being cornered left him no end game.

Not that he was thinking that far ahead, or cared all that much.

"Them cards is *marked*," Swingle said. "That fat man has been winning all day and now I know why. I didn't see nothing until it started to get dark and the boss lady lit the lantern and I could see the marks on his cards. I told him as much and he went for his gun."

The boss lady is Elmira Adler, the owner of the Silver Spoon and my girlfriend. She stood on Carmody's side of the room, the burnt match still in her hand, and the lambency of the lamplight coming to life as it reflected in the gold and silver of her hair.

Swingle's Adam's apple bobbed with rage. It really was an impressive sight, more like an egg than an apple, and it appeared to move the entire length of his neck from the top of his sunken chest to the tip of what little chin he possessed in a face dwarfed by an outsized, drooping mustache.

"Look at them cards!" Swingle commanded, pointing at the dead man, whose mouth was pursed in a circle of surprise, puckered in an eternity of astonishment between his puffy jowls.

No one moved.

"Hold them up to the light!" Swingle said.

Elmira shook her head.

"He can't do that," she said. "He's dead."

Swingle rolled his eyes. I caught myself before I did the same thing.

"I don't mean *him,* for Christ's sake. I mean somebody who ain't dead."

Elmira looked around and determined that she qualified and plucked the cards from the dead man's hand. His fist lifted a couple inches off the table – sometimes people who are killed suddenly clutch things in a death grip – and after it lost its grip, pounded back down on the table in a nasty, alive way.

Everyone in the room jumped, including Swingle.

We all started to breathe again at roughly the same time, and Elmira smoothed her apron and held the cards a couple inches from the wall, next to the coal-oil lantern. The hand was a queen-high flush in spades.

Elmira picked out the queen and leaned in, scrutinizing it with one eye like a jeweler.

"I don't see any marks," she said.

"Not *that* side," Swingle screamed, exasperated, the Adam's apple now dancing like an egg being boiled. "Who in hell marks the sides of cards you're *looking at?*"

I gently told Elmira to turn the card around so we could see the back. She was pushing Swingle to his breaking point. I could tell. I've been there.

"I still don't see a mark," Elmira said.

"I do," I said. "It's like a smudge. You can't see it unless you look at the cards a certain way and then the light doesn't reflect from the smudge."

I asked Elmira to hold up another card from the dead man's hand.

Carmody moved a step closer, ostensibly to get a better look, but I knew he was angling closer to Swingle.

"I see something myself," Carmody said. It came out *ahh see sumpin misself,* in that odd drawl he perfected growing up in a locale where you ate squirrels for breakfast, lunch, and dinner – a part of Tennessee so strange and remote that even non-native squirrels shunned the place.

"It's about an inch from the left, but lower on this card," I said.

Carmody held up a finger, as is his supremely annoying habit, a finger as long and gnarled as a tree branch.

"Now, them smudges might have happened when he squeezed down on the cards when he was getting his brain pan shot out," Carmody said. "Try one from the deck on the table."

Elmira spread the deck out, plucked a card from the middle of the fan, and held it with only the back showing, this time moving it closer to the lamp.

From the back of the room came a round, cultured baritone.

"I am Professor Bosco," said a lean, handsome man with a surgically trimmed mustache and glossy black hair that looked to have been cut and combed one strand at a time.

"And I can tell from here that you are holding the king of spades."

Chapter 3

As I've heard Elmira put it many times, phrasing it in her unique syntax, it was so quiet you could hear the quiet.

It was so silent in the Spoon that I could hear the ringing in my ears produced by Swingle's gunshot. Outside, a dog barked in the distance, a horse pawed the ground, maybe a couple blocks away, and from above, geese honked. There was a surprising amount of activity everywhere except this bar, which was frozen in time as everyone waited.

And waited some more.

"Elmira?" I said, in a whisper, fully aware of the tightly wound homicidal maniac pointing the Colt at my head.

She actually responded by whispering, "Yes?"

Swingle's Adam's apple was about to leap through the top of his skull.

"Honey," I said, speaking slowly and calmly, the way you'd coax a child to change directions after she'd wandered into a bull's pasture, "can you turn the card around?"

"Like this?" she asked, rotating her wrist and displaying the king of spades.

Swingle pivoted the gun toward the man who called himself Professor Bosco.

"You a part of this?" Swingle asked, suddenly calm, showing no expression behind his dead eyes, and displaying the universal demeanor of lunatics everywhere who are about to produce another dead man.

Bosco smiled and chuckled.

He *chuckled.*

Luckily, everyone in the Spoon was standing up. Otherwise, Swingle might have been startled by the sound of jaws hitting the table.

Bosco spread his hands and tilted his head, shaking it gently from side to side. He smiled like my uncle used to do when I was a little kid and asked a dumb question.

"No, of course not," he said. "I am Professor Bosco, a conjurer, and Mrs. Adler has booked my traveling show to play in your beautiful amphitheater starting on Monday. I had just arrived when the commotion began. Forgive me for not making my presence known sooner."

Elmira brightened.

"Hello, Professor Bosco," she said, and gave him a full-arm wave from all of ten feet away.

Swingle's eyes narrowed and his grip tightened on the Colt. I could see the constriction in the ridges on the back of his hand.

"What in hell's a *con-joo-yer?*"

Bosco's theatrical baritone filled the room.

"A prestidigitator, sir. A player of tricks. I can appear to read minds, make voices appear from nowhere and everywhere through the process of ventriloquism, saw women in half and rejoin them, and – as you'll see next week – rob men of their strength so that they cannot lift a box that weighs no more than five pounds."

"You're a magician, you mean," Swingle said.

Bosco flashed the patient-uncle smile again.

"'Magic' is the realm of the superstitious, sir. This is the nineteenth century! The modern conjurer is an illusionist. I make no claim to dark powers. I do, however, promise to astound you and confound you with my skill."

I was actually getting drawn into Bosco's patter but there was, after all, a dead man in the room and a lunatic waving a gun, and I felt professionally obligated to get things back on track.

"So you know about marked cards?" I said.

"My specialty. I do many card tricks. It's called 'close-up illusion.'"

"Tell us more," I said.

I noticed that Swingle's eyes were locked on Bosco and I inched a little closer to the gunman as Bosco held forth. I wanted to grab the weapon. While I could probably draw my pistol and shoot Swingle when he looked away, even mortally wounded men have been known to fire off all six shots, and there were probably thirty people in the room.

"What you've fallen victim to," Bosco continued, "is a simple scheme, though it is well-executed in this case. The person who marked the cards placed a small scuff, the position of which, moving from left to right, indicates the suit. I saw from the other cards that the scuff was at the far left, and it was a spade, so I could tell that what Mrs. Adler was holding was a spade. I would guess the pattern is probably spade, club, heart, and diamond. The distance of the scuff down from the *top* of the card indicates its rank. Usually only face cards are marked this way. The top is ace, then king, and so on."

I'd known Snake Swingle since the war, and while he's crazy he's not stupid, and I think he came to his realization a second before I did. Anyway, I was in trouble.

He turned his gun back on me.

"These cards is supplied by the *house*," Swingle said. "And you and the boss lady own the place. Hawke, you're a goddamn crook."

And I could see the nail of his trigger finger whiten as he applied more pressure.

Chapter 4

In a way, it made things simpler. There was no one directly in back of Snake, so I didn't have to worry about a stray shot striking a patron. And while I didn't turn my head, I could hear the shuffling of patrons behind me who didn't want to share my fate and were clearing out of the path of any bullets that might miss or travel through me.

The only complication was that he was holding the old Colt level at my chest while my expensive new single-action Smith and Wesson Schofield was still lounging in its holster. My only hope was to stage a distraction so I could drop, roll, and shoot.

As if on cue, Bosco spoke up.

"I wouldn't be too quick to blame the house," Bosco said.

Swingle relaxed but kept his eyes locked on me. He was an experienced killer – an attribute that once, to my ultimate regret, worked in my favor – and wasn't easily distracted.

"The house generally has little to gain from marked cards in poker," Bosco said. "The house takes a cut of the pot so it doesn't matter to them who wins. Most likely the marked deck was planted."

Swingle wasn't buying it.

"All the cards here is the same. How'd the fat asshole get hold of them unless Hawke or the Boss Lady gave them to him?"

"May I see some packs from your unopened stock?" Bosco said.

Elmira's eyes moved to me, and I nodded. Swingle's eyes stayed fixed on the general location of my yet-unperforated heart. And Carmody almost imperceptibly edged yet another step closer to Swingle.

Elmira slipped through the door to the back office and returned in what seemed like no longer than a week with an armful of decks, which she deposited like a mudslide on the table in front of Bosco. Bosco broke the seals on two of the decks with his thumb and made a face like there was a bad smell in the room.

"Perchance can you be good enough to tell me from where you purchased the cards?" Bosco said.

"*Perchance can you be good enough to tell me,*" Swingle parroted. "Who in hell talks like that? *Perchance?* What kind of game are you guys playing?"

"I understand your concern, good sir," Bosco said.

"Kiss my ass, good sir," Swingle said.

"Atlas Novelty and Supply," Elmira said. "In Austin."

And then Bosco stepped directly between me and Swingle, not three feet from the little psychotic's muzzle, holding an opened deck in his left hand and pointing to it with his right.

I saw Carmody's eyes widen slightly, which for him is the equivalent of a normal man having a seizure. Swingle, at a rare loss for words, stared and shook his head.

"A double layer of glue," Bosco intoned, as though it meant something to anyone.

Actually, it meant something to Carmody. Bosco had Swingle's attention and Carmody was able to move forward another inch.

"I'm listening," Swingle said. "And just so you know, I loaded these cartridges myself and they're strong enough so I can shoot right through both of you, which I will sure as hell do if your ape deputy sneaks up any closer."

Carmody scowled.

"You have great presence of mind and awareness of your situation, sir," Bosco said. "You would make an excellent conjurer. And if I could be so bold, I wager you are experienced in combat and successful in its execution."

And then I realized that Bosco had set the hook and was playing the little man. The pretentious son of a bitch really knew how to work a room.

"As a matter of fact," Swingle said, "I was one of only a thousand men to win the Medal of Honor, presented to me personal by President Lincoln, and I got it for saving the life of that sorry swindler who's hiding behind you."

Bosco stepped aside slightly, nodded toward me, and told Swingle he was sure I was grateful and all Americans were in his debt, and so forth.

Bosco kept ladling it on until he had the little lunatic puffed up and damn near hypnotized.

"And as to the cards," Bosco said, "what typically happens in a case like we have here is that someone will buy a gross of decks from a supplier and find a ruse to return them the next day, saying, perhaps, that they were the wrong color. The packs appear unopened, but during the night the perpetrator has opened them, marked them, and resealed them."

Swingle nodded.

"From there, it's a simple matter of either finding out through subterfuge which establishment bought the marked decks or simply traveling to casinos in the area until the person who marked the decks finds them in play."

Elmira held up her hand like a schoolgirl.

"How can you tell these were tampered with?"

Bosco held the box up above his head, playing to an invisible balcony.

"Because I see two different types of glue on the flap that seals the box. One is white and flaky, probably a glue made from milk, but the other is yellowish, which I think is based on a wax of some sort. In this part of the country, I imagine it would be candelilla wax, distilled from a common weed. No one would know that the flap had been released unless they knew what to look for. And what to *smell* for."

Swingle was enraptured and asked Bosco what he meant.

"Candelilla wax," Bosco said, "has a strong sulfuric smell, even after it's long dried. I could smell it when I picked up the first pack, and the smell is obviously inconsistent with the flaky white milk paste, and no manufacturer would find reason to glue anything shut with two different compounds. But you needn't take my word for it."

And he handed the deck to Swingle, who snorted at it like a curious pig.

"Smells like shit," Swingle said.

I was about to make my move when Swingle came out of his trance.

"Wait a minute," he said. "You talk a good game but how do I know you ain't just serving up flapdoodle? Anybody can make up a story like you just done. How do I know you really is some expert on cards? Prove it."

"May I have the deck, sir?"

Swingle handed it over.

"Prove it," Swingle said.

Bosco extracted the cards, letting the box fall to the floor. He cut the deck into halves, and fanned them out in each hand, creating perfect circles. Re-forming the deck, he squeezed the edges and shot a waterfall of cards two feet from one hand to the other. And then he spread the deck from palm to shoulder and flipped it from the bottom up, the cards turning over in a slow crawl up his arm.

"That'll work," Swingle said.

"And now," Bosco said, "may I suggest you lower your firearm? I'm sure the marshal will treat you fairly."

"The marshal will beat me 'til I'm worm food."

"I'm sure he'll act reasonably, Bosco said. "Right now you're in a hopeless situation, what with that man covering you from above."

I could see Swingle's wheels turning. In one part of his brain, he probably knew that the Spoon's ceiling was flat and only about fifteen feet high and there were no skylights or beams, so it wasn't possible for anyone to be above him.

Still, humans are bred to fear a threat from above.

Swingle wanted to look up, but didn't.

Bosco looked up, looked down, and looked right at Swingle.

Then the voice said, "Drop it, or I'll shoot you right through the top of your thick skull."

Chapter 5

S wingle looked up the way you do when you don't really want to see what might be there. Say, when you're in a room full of cobwebs and you feel something furry on your forehead.

That's when I dove for the gun. Literally, I dove: I was a foot or so above and horizontal to the floor when I grabbed it and began wrestling. I wanted to knock it to the ground, but Swingle was fast and surprisingly strong for somebody built like a pipe cleaner, and he wrestled it partially out of my grip and pulled the trigger.

He knew guns. He knew that if he fired it, even into the floor, the splinters would distract me and the barrel would likely become too hot for me to keep my grip.

Even when a gun is cocked, the hammer still comes back a fraction of an inch when the trigger starts to pull so when I moved my grip up the barrel and grabbed the body of the gun I had some room to stick the web of skin between my thumb and forefinger beneath the hammer.

The hammer clamped down painfully but harmlessly.

Then Carmody grabbed Swingle's wrist, which was tantamount to squeezing the wrist in a vice and then setting the vice in concrete. Swingle knew he couldn't wrest himself away from Carmody's grip, and gave up.

When I regained my feet, the Colt was still dangling from my hand like an animal that had bitten my hand and latched on. I thumbed the hammer back gently, keeping the barrel pointed toward the floor, and disengaged myself.

Swingle, with Carmody's huge hand still wrapped around all of his wrist and half of his forearm, sighed and shut his eyes.

"All right, Hawke," he said, "I know what you're gonna do, so get it over with."

And with that I laid the barrel of his gun alongside his head.

Chapter 6

Carmody, Elmira and I had a drink in the back room after I'd placed the body of the man Swingle shot in our official town morgue, which is the corner of my office most distant from my desk.

Official policy, which around here basically means whatever I decided to do most recently, is that we keep a body for a day, waiting to see if anybody claims it or if we can notify next of kin. Or if we've made a mistaken diagnosis and it comes back to life.

The portly gambler carried no identification but quite a bit of money – more than $300. That posed a practical and ethical dilemma because presumably some of that wad of cash was money he'd won earlier in the day by cheating people.

Normally, unclaimed money goes into the general fund for the marshal's office, paying for ammunition, fees, and salaries. While I bend a rule here and there, I'm careful about documenting all the money and keep it in the safe. When I find pictures of family and Bibles and such I keep them in the safe, too. They meant something to somebody once, and it's not my job to throw them away.

My drink in the back room wasn't very relaxing. Carmody had one of his laughing fits, during which he generally coughs and slaps his knee and brays like some species of barnyard animal.

"Never seen nobody so relieved as when you was able to hide behind that Bosco character," Carmody said, snorting into the back of his hand, trying to keep his whiskey from exiting through his nose.

"And then you was staring up at the ceiling like everybody else when he threw his voice. You'd still be standing there slack-jawed if I hadn't grabbed the little weasel."

I let it pass, as I usually do with most of Carmody's remanufactured versions of events. He's saved my life more than I've saved his so I figure he's entitled to a little fun at my expense.

Aside from that, if I tried to chew him out I was pretty sure I'd start laughing myself.

"How did he do that?" Elmira said. Her mountain-lake-blue eyes were wide with a childlike wonder one doesn't see often in a woman in her early 40s, which was our best guess as to her age. She'd been taken by Apaches when she was a child and escaped when she was a young woman, and nobody kept much in the way of records in the interim.

Elmira had been married to the original owner of the Silver Spoon, which is a moderately successful if somewhat shabby bar, bordello, and gambling house in Shadow Valley, which is a shabby little town in the ass end of nowhere. But it's a place not without its charms, including Elmira.

She inherited the place when her husband was murdered by her daughter – a story for another time – and brought me to Shadow Valley at the behest of the former marshal, Billy Gannon.

Gannon had been captain of my unit during the war, and when things started getting inexplicably squirrely in Shadow Valley he'd asked Elmira to contact me if anything happened to him. Something did happen to him, and it involved three bullets to the side of his head.

It would have taken a very tough man to kill Billy Gannon.

The killer's name was Purcell, and he *was* tough, and smart, and vicious, and quick.

And now he's dead because I tracked him down and killed him.

In the process I sort of inherited Gannon's job.

I suddenly realized that I'd been looking at Elmira, marveling at those eyes, and had forgotten to respond to the question.

"He explained it to me when I wrote up the report," I said. "He said he'd learned a lot of stage business as a magician, including ventriloquism. You learn to talk without moving your lips. You can say most sounds without moving your lips, but the ones you can't, you substitute with sounds that are close and if you practice, it sounds like normal speech."

Elmira stayed focused on me, bathing me with all her attention, like a kid listening to a bed-time story.

"But how'd he throw his voice?"

"You can't really throw a voice," Carmody said. "It's a trick. It's misdirection. But I ain't no expert in sneaky stuff. Let the master explain."

I let that pass, too, but for the record, Carmody was right. I was an officer during the war – a transgression for which Carmody, a sergeant, has never forgiven me – and I was attached to a unit specializing in what were called "special tactics" or "dirty tricks," the designation depending on whether you were doing them or having them done to you.

"Tom's right," I said, "as he is on rare occasions. People just aren't very good at locating sound. You rely on your eyes to cue you where the sound comes from."

"Tell her one of your war-hero stories," Carmody said, transparently stifling a yawn. "Get it over with."

Elmira nodded and her eyes got wider and she smiled and urged me on.

What could I do?

"Illusion is a big part of wartime strategy," I said.

"Should we take notes?" Carmody said.

I ignored him.

"So let me tell you how Sergeant Carmody probably saved the lives of a score of men when he was a scout for the Tennessee Union Volunteers."

That shut him up.

"I wasn't there," I said, "I never encountered Tom during the war but soldiers talk and I've heard tell of the time he fooled a Reb contingent into retreating from a valley. It was getting dark, and Union forces were shelling from the east. The artillery was high up on the side of a hill. The Rebs weren't happy but they kept moving through the lowland and stayed near the hill to the west, as far away from the cannons as they could without getting into the scrub on the other slope. Tom led a squad of scouts up the hill on the other side of the valley and they lit small fires and hid them by holding blankets in front of them."

I stood and pantomimed a toreador sweep of a cape.

"When the cannon to the east went off," I said, "the Union troops on the west side swept the blankets aside and the rebs in the valley thought they were seeing muzzle flashes from the west, too. They thought they were whipsawed in a crossfire and retreated. There were a couple hundred of them, and they would probably have massacred the Union troops they were chasing if they had kept on going."

Elmira clapped her hands in delight and Carmody cleared his throat and took a sudden interest in his fingernails.

"The point," I said, "is that in most cases you really can't tell where sound is coming from, and your mind will tell you the sound is coming from where your *eyes* tell you it's coming from. That's why Bosco looked up a second before he did the ventriloquism bit, and then he changed his voice and made it a little softer like it was a different person coming from farther away. Your mind plays tricks."

Elmira nodded and turned to Carmody, less interested in Bosco now and focused on the shiny new story about Carmody.

"Tom, I know you don't like to talk about yourself much," she said. "And Josiah doesn't talk about the war except when somebody asks him point blank and then of course he can't stop himself, but that's a *great* story. Is that really what happened?"

"More or less," Carmody said.

"Should we have taken notes?" I asked.

Chapter 7

I saw Bosco the next day at Elmira's combination church, theater, and meeting-hall, where he was setting up for his show. Elmira had purchased the shop next to the Silver Spoon and convinced Carmody and me to tear the shop down and build a new structure to her exact specifications, which included punishingly tight seating.

She was instinctively a sharp businesswoman and calculated what she called the "ass capacity" that would enable the addition to pay for itself. She recognized that a church stood empty except for Sunday mornings, and was generally half-empty even then, but she also knew that churches and schools were essential if the community were to grow.

We have a circuit preacher who rides in to save souls on Sunday, in what possibly could be the only church in the West, or the country, or the world, for that matter, that shares a common wall with a whorehouse.

The rest of the time Elmira books various traveling acts for her venue. While Shadow Valley isn't exactly on the way to much of anything, we're not far from Austin and San Antonio and she's able to get some pretty good troupes, many of which migrated this way from San Francisco, which I understand has become pretty much the entertainment capital of the West.

Bosco was assembling some boards that created an elevated stage, which I thought was pointless because there already was an elevated stage and he was putting another one on top of it, but I'm not one to tell a man his business.

He seemed startled to see me, as did the woman with him, a lithe and dark-haired beauty wearing, of all things, *pants*.

"Marshal Hawke," he said, and actually bowed. I wondered if he ever let up on the act, but again, it's not for me to tell him his business.

"I want to thank you for your hospitality," he said, "and introduce you to my wife, Gina."

Gina, I estimated, was no more than 25 and despite the masculine cut of her garb she filled it out perfectly and in abundance and in all the right places.

"*Ciao*," she said, and stuck out her hand.

It took me a second to decide whether she was hungry and asking for food or saying hello in Italian. I took a gamble and told her *ciao* back.

I was going to say something else in Italian but then I remembered that I didn't know anything else.

So we stood there for a while.

"Can I do anything for you, Marshal?" Bosco said.

"No, in fact I came to see if there was anything you needed. Whatever I can do to help, I will. You may have saved my life yesterday."

Gina nodded.

"*Sì*, I hear how you hide behind him," she said.

At least I knew she spoke English.

Bosco broke in quickly.

"That's not how it happened, Gina, and you didn't hear that from me."

Gina nodded again.

"No, I hear that from big tall deputy with beard like wire brush," Gina said. "He come by about an hour ago."

Before I could respond I saw the movement out of the corner of my eye.

I held up my left hand and put my right on the butt of my sidearm.

Bosco saw my alarm and told me that my caution wasn't necessary. But in my business I'm allergic to people hiding on me so I took three steps and swept the stage curtain aside and confronted...Gina.

She took a second to compose herself, wiped some dust off her very tight pants, and said, *"Ciao."*

I looked back at Bosco who was standing next to the *other* Gina and he sighed and said he should probably explain things.

I said that was an excellent idea and we all sat on the half-built stage and he told me the damnedest story I'd ever heard.

And that covers a lot of territory.

Chapter 8

He was neither a professor nor an Italian, although I had already guessed that much.

His real name will William Guillaume, he told me, a legacy reflecting his French-Canadian father's oddball sense of humor, as Guillaume is the French version of the name William.

It's pronounced the American-style way, he told me, *Guh-YOME*. But if it was all the same to me he'd rather just be called Bosco.

I couldn't see any harm in that, I told him, and asked him if Bosco was supposed to be his first or last name. He shrugged and said it didn't matter.

The mysterious Professor Bosco hailed from the exotic locale of Newark, New Jersey. He grew up there and as a teenager was apprenticed to his uncle as a watchmaker. Bosco turned out to be something of a watchmaking prodigy. In fact, Bosco became so skilled in the mysteries of gears and springs that he began building and selling mechanized toys before he turned twenty. Having a flair for art, he fashioned a bird out of metal and rigged it so it could convincingly chirp and flutter its wings. He sold dozens of them and was able to buy more tools and parts.

Bosco progressed to increasingly elaborate machines and in a year or so built a mechanical torso with an arm that gripped a pen and could write short phrases. The device was a hit at local carnivals and Bosco was able to sell versions to wealthy collectors, novelty dealers, and to a touring magician named LoPresti.

LoPresti, who really *was* Italian, expanded on the machine's repertoire by having it write answers to questions posed by the audience. The mechanical man's most impressive trick was having its hand covered by a scarf, and on LoPresti's command, writing out the suit and rank of a playing card. Then, a member of the audience would pick a card from a deck proffered by the magician.

Invariably the card drawn was the jack of clubs, and LoPresti would sweep away the scarf to reveal that the mechanical man had written *jack of clubs* on the paper.

Of course LoPresti's entire deck consisted of 52 jacks of clubs and of course he would palm the deck and substitute a real deck *missing* the jack of clubs. LoPresti would display the real deck to the audience after the fact, assuring them that there was no trickery involved.

It was Bosco's job to pose as a member of the audience and demand to see the deck, and then to stomp away in a huff when LoPresti foiled him.

Bosco was an able magician's apprentice and picked up the patter and the sleight of hand readily. When LoPresti toured Europe, he brought Bosco along, and sometimes Bosco would substitute for The Great LoPresti when the master was too drunk or too hung over to perform – and it became obvious to all that Bosco was surpassing his master, not merely in the technical performance but also with his skill with manipulating and captivating an audience.

And then Bosco struck out on his own. The market for conjurers was both shrinking and oversupplied in Europe, but America was the land of opportunity and Bosco returned to it, working his way west.

I had one more question, of course. Why were there two Ginas? Why did one of them hide from me? I didn't ask, but I was also curious about whether he was married to both of them.

Bosco told me he really had to prepare for his evening performance and put his hand on my shoulder and ushered me toward the door.

Gina and Louisa, he explained, were twins. Twin girls – especially distractingly beautiful ones – were coveted in the conjuring business and could always find work on the circuit. One twin of them could "reappear" at will once the other one, for example, scooted through a trap door in the back of a box where she was supposedly confined.

Sometimes, Bosco said, if one twin were especially provocative the other could walk off stage virtually in plain sight, merely covering herself in a cloth the same color as the background as camouflage.

It was all about distraction.

I'd lost my train of thought thinking about the special outfits the girls would wear to distract the audience, and when I snapped back I asked Bosco why the other girl hid from me.

Naturally, Bosco said, if word got out that Bosco's assistant had a twin sister the effect would be ruined, and that's why Louisa had scuttled behind the curtain.

Bosco held the door for me.

I surrendered to my curiosity and asked whether he was married to them both. Not that I was looking to enforce any bigamy laws, I assured him. I just wondered.

Bosco gave me that chuckle again and said he really wasn't married and that conjurers often claimed that their assistants were their wives to simplify booking hotel rooms.

I couldn't help myself.

I asked him if he shared his room with both of them.

He gave me that chuckle again.

"It's not what you think," he said.

"It is much, *much* better than what you imagine," he said, and shut the door behind me.

Chapter 9

If I hadn't spent the next ten minutes staring off into the distance musing about precisely what Bosco meant, I might not have seen them coming.

In my glassy-eyed reverie, I happened to be looking in the right direction to pick up what looked to be a cloud of dust through a clearing that was probably two miles away. One of the strategic advantages of being in a valley between some fairly steep hills is that your surroundings are tipped up and on display.

But I needed some sharper eyes to figure out what was happening, so I tracked down Carmody in the Spoon, where he was dealing Faro. It's not so much that Carmody can see more detail – my eyesight is pretty good, but his is remarkable – it's the fact that he can read movements and terrain like you or I read a newspaper.

Carmody retrieved a brass spyglass but didn't use it for the first five minutes he spent staring at the hills in the direction I'd indicated.

"If you saw a cloud from this distance, it probably means at least six riders," he said, squinting into the sun. "Given the fact that your eyes ain't good enough for you to count your own toes, I'd say it must be a substantial group if you saw what you claim you did."

I was about to say something when Carmody went on point like a dog.

"Birds," he said.

"Birds," I repeated.

"Yep."

"There are birds in the air. Who the hell cares?"

"You ain't never going to get it," he said. It came out, *ya ain't niver gonna git it.* "Can you see that flock of starlings about ten degrees below where you claim you saw the dust?"

"Of course," I lied.

"Don't it make you suspicious how they swoop down and then dart up sudden like that?"

"They encountered something they didn't expect," I said, with the same sense of validation I had when I was able to solve math problems in school and win the approval of my stern teacher.

"There's a trail under the tree canopy where the birds is. That same trail comes into plain sight down near that rock ledge. If they're coming this way, I'll be able to see them."

Carmody put the glass to his left eye, holding it with both hands. Puzzled, he looked at the glass and moved it to his right eye.

He seemed satisfied.

We don't know exactly how old Carmody is, either, but we think he's a couple years older than I am, and I'm 44. Maybe his eyeballs are starting to wear out, too. At least the left one.

We waited, and I became aware of the buzz of insects and the puffing of a gentle wind as Carmody stood like a statue.

"I was right," he said.

"Right about what?"

"Six riders. Youngish men and one older. Rifles in scabbards."

A group of armed men could be traveling through for a lot of inconsequential or innocent reasons. A hunting party, maybe, or a posse from another town, or a group of cattlemen pursing a rustler.

Or a traveling chess team or six well-armed preachers coming to share the word.

Carmody and I both headed to the office to get our rifles.

We didn't live to be old enough for our eyes to go bad by being optimists.

Chapter 10

I keep a chain looped through the trigger guards
of the rifles and of course I keep it padlocked
and of course the damn lock always gets fussy
when I'm in a hurry.

To make the day even a little better, the body
in the corner was starting to smell and Snake
Swingle was banging on the bars and I was getting a
serious headache.

"I am aggrieved," he shouted, pounding on
the iron, which resonated with a surprisingly musi-
cal hum. *"Aggrieved!"*

"Snake," I said, trying to get the key to catch,
"we don't have a lot of time here."

"Don't call me 'Snake.'"

"If I was named Seymour," Carmody said,
pushing me aside and having a go at the lock, "I'd
opt for 'Snake.'"

"My daddy was named Seymour," Swingle
said, "and if it was good enough for him, it's good
enough for me. And my point is that I didn't do
nothing wrong. Let me out. I'm innocent and I've
gotta pee."

Carmody got the lock open and extricated my
lever-action Winchester, not the most powerful rifle

in the world – or even in my rack – but light, agile, and dependable. Carmody knows my preferences and sometimes does my thinking for me when we're pressed for time. I guessed that he would opt for his big-bore shotgun, and I was right.

"You blew somebody's brains out," Carmody said, "and you're a homicidal maniac."

"He drew on me first," Swingle said.

That wasn't exactly the way I'd heard it – the shooting sounded like a mutual attempt at homicide, which was won, as is usually the case, by the most maniacal maniac. But Swingle had a point. I wasn't sure I could charge him with anything. The fat gambler *had* pulled a gun, and there's no local ordinance or state law that allows for locking up maniacs on general principles.

And, of course, Swingle had waded into enemy fire a dozen years ago to save my life.

"I'm innocent and I gotta pee!" he screamed. "And I can reach your damn desk from here. Don't you think I can't. I got a pecker like a fire hose. So it's up to you, Hawke."

I tossed the key ring through the bars as Carmody and I ran out the door.

I had an important letter on that desk and I didn't want it to get wet.

Chapter 11

I rode directly toward the end of the trail, and
Carmody rode toward a slope that would overlook the higher portions of the path. It would be
tricky riding through brush and rocks, but Carmody
– who has assembled an impressive collection of
mounts, funded by his horse-trading abilities –
stopped at the stable and retrieved what he called his
"mountain horse." It was a small, slow-moving
breed with an unusual gait that kept at least one hoof
on the ground even when it ran flat-out, and as a result it was remarkably sure-footed.

While Carmody saddled up the barrel-chested
brown rock-monkey, I poked my head into the
Spoon and told Elmira as little as possible, just that
there were some unidentified riders coming down
the hill and that Carmody and I were going to meet
them.

Her face froze over and she nodded, giving
me that curt bob of the head that told me that while
she understood that it had to be done, she suspected
that I secretly enjoyed putting myself in the line of
fire and somehow did it to spite her.

I can't blame her, and I hated to see her worried, but there was no spite involved or intended. As

to the first part of her grievance, she might have a point.

In this case, I had no choice but to offer myself up. I'd be safer letting them ride in and confronting them from a rooftop or behind a building, but then the fight, if there was one, would be in the middle of town, endangering innocent citizens, and I'm obligated to avoid that.

I'm not really sure we have any innocent citizens, but a job is a job.

I rode off first, hoping to draw their attention while Carmody scuttled invisibly in a broad circle through the scrub. No riders had emerged from the tree canopy yet when I pulled away, and as I put distance between myself and the town I was puzzled not to hear hoofbeats from Carmody's plodding mountain horse.

I risked one quick look back, though I really didn't want to. The last thing I wanted to do was divert their attention to Carmody.

Carmody was standing in the stirrups, surveying the hill, slowly shaking his head, and I got the impression that something was very wrong but now everything was in motion and I didn't dare look back again.

Chapter 12

The older man, who was in the lead, didn't seem surprised to see me.

He reined his mount, a lanky chestnut Morgan, to a halt about twenty feet in front of me and said they were just there to talk. The five others filled in a circle around me. They were kids, tough-looking, but they still had not outgrown the category of unskilled labor, I surmised. They were nervous and looked at each other too quickly and too often and they betrayed their inexperience by arranging themselves so that they were in each other's line of fire.

The older one, a sturdy fellow with gray swept-back hair and long sideburns, swept back like wings, took pains to show he was in no hurry. He lit a small cigar, puffed on it, and regarded it thoughtfully. In a second or two I could smell it, a leathery tang mixing beguilingly with the aroma of nearby pine needles and the dried grass.

As I had nothing to do but wait while he played his game, I asked him if I he had an extra.

A couple of the riders started to laugh but Sideburns silenced them with a hard look, shrugged, and fished a cigar out of his vest pocket. He made it clear I'd have to come to him and fetch it, so I did, and he handed it to me.

I didn't have a match so I asked him for a light.

I was more than content to play the make-the-other-guy-sweat game because I had no other options at the moment. I needed to stall until Carmody arrived, and, besides that, the cigar was actually very good. I had a feeling Sideburns was accustomed to the finer things in life; his stately Morgan probably cost as much as a small house and his hat looked to be the glossy beaver variety that would cost a regular trail hand three months' wages, which is the reason you never see them on the heads of regular trail hands.

While I don't use tobacco as a habit, I'll indulge every once in a while.

The cigar was very strong, though, and I was getting a little dizzy as I waited for Carmody to signal me that he was in position. I knew I wouldn't hear him moving and didn't waste my energy trying. Carmody would dismount at a discreet distance, I knew, and cover the remaining territory on foot. He could slink like a jungle cat and glide through brush without snapping a twig or rustling a leaf.

So I waited and smoked coughed a few times. Nothing.

We hadn't discussed what signal Carmody would use to alert me that he was in place but we'd worked together long enough so that I knew his repertoire. In a clearing surrounded by trees, he'd probably imitate the throaty chirp of a scrub jay – a squawk you hear day and night in most parts of this territory, but Carmody would do it twice in short succession, a rhythm no self-respecting scrub jay actually performs.

Sideburns apparently was getting tired of the game and stubbed the butt out on the pommel of his saddle and threw it into the bushes. It was the unconscious, habitual action of a smart man accustomed to covering his tracks, and that was the first of his actions that actually worried me.

I normally enjoy working with people who are good at what they do except when I suspect they are looking to kill me.

"You're Hawke," he said.

It wasn't a question, so I didn't answer.

"The Man wants me to give you a message."

So it was like this, I thought. *The Man.* A self-important local gangster, I presumed. Every wide spot in the road has one.

I flicked my cigar butt into some dry grass a few feet from Sideburns. I'm not one to be reckless with fire, but with Carmody missing in action I might soon be sorely in need of a distraction.

"I figured you'd meet us on the way," Sideburns said. "Wanting to protect your girlfriend. Elmira, her name is? Don't blame you. She's a beautiful woman, be a shame if something happened to her. Good that she has somebody like you around."

I noticed that brushfire had fizzled and apparently so had Carmody. I was on my own.

"You came all this way so 'The Man' could threaten a woman?" I said.

"Nobody's making threats," Sideburns said. "I'm here to make you an offer."

He reached into his pocket and pulled out two cigars and was about to offer me one when we heard the volley of gunshots from the valley.

Chapter 13

Sideburns was paralyzed with indecision. Whatever was unfolding down in the valley was not in his script.

His hired help were perplexed, too, and they retreated to the universal routine of low-level thugs out of their depth – looking around for somebody to tell them what to do.

As horses are wont to do, they sensed the uncertainty, and in an instant the clearing was alive with sound: the flat thudding of their nervous footfalls, a whinny, a disgusted obscenity from Sideburns, more gunfire from the valley, and a double warble from a scrub jay.

A song no scrub jay actually sings.

I drew my sidearm while Sideburns was trying to settle his horse.

I caught him by surprise and he held up one hand, palm out, while clutching the reins with the other.

"There wasn't supposed to be gunplay," Sideburns said, as though that explained it all. Then he told me to put down my gun because I was outnumbered and there was no reason for me to aim at him, anyway.

Next, of course, the slack-jawed idiot to my left felt it necessary to claw for his pistol and I pivoted and shot him in the head.

At that moment I did not want to shoot any more idiots. I wanted nothing more than to ride back into town. My duty, my girlfriend, and the handful of people I call friends were all there, all being bombarded with what sounded like a regiment of infantry.

But my options for trying to get back to town were severely limited. As soon as I turned to ride, I'd be shot in the back. I suppose I could try to back the horse up all the way, which might get me there in a day or so. Or I could shoot it out with the remaining five.

Sideburns made the decision for me. He sprung to action after I turned toward the idiot and I caught the glint of a long nickel-plated barrel as he drew and hunched low behind the Morgan's crest, using the mount's head for cover.

I'd swiveled ninety degrees and had too far to turn back if I were going to get off a shot at Sideburns, and my only option – and not a very good one – was to throw myself in back of my horse, hit the ground, and scramble.

I was about to try it when I heard the concussive roar and Sideburns was swept off his horse, as though with an invisible hand.

***

They always get it wrong in the stage plays, where the bad guy gets shot with a handgun and flies backward. Most people, when they're shot with a ball or a bullet, just fall straight down because the round goes right through them. Sometimes they fall forward when a bullet expands in their head and blows brains out the rear, the same way a pumpkin falls toward you if you shoot it off a fencepost.

But a shotgun delivers a spread-out surface blast, and does blast a body back, and Carmody favors small shot and massive charges that he loads himself into a gun that the smith reinforced and re-chambered to accommodate the huge load.

The short version of the story is that Sideburns would not be a threat, ever. He was, in fact, a few gory threads away from being in two pieces.

Sideburns' horse actually cranked his head back and pivoted, trying to figure out where his rider had gone. Horses are like people. Some people freeze in shock. Others wander in puzzled circles.

The four remaining gunmen panicked, spurred their mounts, and took off the way they came. I could probably have hit at least two of them in the back before they rode behind cover, and Carmody could certainly have shredded the others from his perch, but we had other things on our minds.

We headed back to town at a full gallop.

Chapter 14

I've never seen too many photographs close-up before but a few months ago a bar patron was showing off a framed tintype of himself big-game hunting. I thought it was odd that somebody traveling through these parts would take the trouble to lug the thing around – tintypes are heavy, and they're actually printed on steel, not tin – much less go through the trouble of hiring a photographer to follow him around until he managed to shoot a bear. But I try not to judge.

I thought of that photo, the self-satisfied smile, the jaunty angle of the rifle barrel, the up-raised foot on the fallen prey, as soon as I rode around the corner on Front Street and saw Snake Swingle.

My mount, a fast quarterhorse called a Steeldust, had covered the half-mile or so back to town in less than two minutes, I reckoned. And I hadn't heard a shot in about half that time.

Meaning that Swingle had needed only a minute to drag five bodies into a heap and stand astride the pile in triumph.

The street had emptied of sane people, which left Elmira, the blacksmith, the druggist, and Bosco.

The blacksmith, a brawny young man name of Richard Oak, had seen a little combat during the war and he'd helped me out on occasion, displaying a big heart but limited skills with his beloved .22, sort of a toy that could conceivably drop a squirrel if the squirrel happened to be of a dainty species. Oak was leaning on the .22 and shaking his head.

The druggist, Vern Miller, was a sour old man who always looked like he'd just finished sucking a pickle, and as best I can determine he'd seen more gunfire than any man would care to, during at least two wars. He'd helped me out on occasion, too, and he favored a big German rifle, upon which he also leaned now.

Miller looked at me, shook his head, and shrugged.

Bosco held both palms up and raised his eyebrows and shook his head. Gina or Louisa popped her head out the door, and then retracted it like a turtle so that the other Gina or Louisa could poke her head out.

I dismounted and ran to Elmira, who had both hands covering her mouth, her fingertips partially covering her eyes, which were as wide as saucers. You could see the whites all the way around the round blue orbs.

Behind me, I could hear Carmody's overburdened little trail horse pounding toward us.

"Are there any other hostiles?" I said to no one in particular.

"They're all there," Elmira said, pointing to the pile.

I turned to Carmody and waved my hands and shouted to him that it was all clear. Then I asked no one in particular what the hell happened.

"We just got here," Oak said, "when he was piling up the bodies."

"He dragged them all by himself," Elmira said.

"Little bastard's stronger than he looks," Miller added.

Chapter 15

Elmira doesn't drink much. Being around the stuff day in and day out sort of kills her appetite for it, she says, but today she insisted she needed a couple to calm down.

Elmira, Carmody, and I sat at the only table in the Spoon that remained upright. The place looked like a hurricane had swept through.

"They came in a few minutes after you left," she said, pouring herself another shot. She drank it daintily, with her little finger pointed skyward, and then smeared her sleeve across her mouth in a gesture that I'd have more readily expected from Carmody.

"Tom stopped by all in a lather and told me something might be up," she said.

"I wasn't in no lather," Carmody said. "Just in a hurry. I had to look after you and hightail back to save Josiah, and it's good I did 'cause the first thing he did was get hisself surrounded. But I knew something was up."

I started to ask him how, but Elmira seemed anxious to recount the events so she could purge them from her mind.

"Tom told me to send a girl to get Richard and Vern," Elmira said, "and for me to leave through the back. But that gang was here in no time at all. Started roughing up the barmaid and tipping over chairs and tables. One of them knew me – I don't know how because I didn't know him – and he told me this was only a taste of what was coming. Then they started busting up the place."

She poured another shot but her hand was shaking and most of it pooled on the table. Carmody took the bottle and poured for her, and then asked me if I wanted some. I'm not much of an afternoon drinker so I declined. Carmody apparently gave an instant's thought to getting a glass but, exhausted by the prospect of hunting through the rubble, he just wrapped those squirrel-eating lips around the lip of the bottle and tipped it up.

Elmira downed her shot daintily and drew her sleeve across her chin again.

Carmody tipped the bottle toward her and asked if she wanted a refill and Elmira stared with some ill-disguised unease at the place where he'd just affixed those lips and politely declined.

She took a deep breath and continued.

"It all happened so fast. They were wrecking the place one minute and then Professor Bosco showed up waving a hammer and told them he'd crack their skulls. He sounds different when he's mad. Uses a lot of words I didn't expect a professor from Italy would know."

I told her that he wasn't really from Italy but it wasn't important now.

"So one of them pulled a gun on Professor Bosco. Another of them said to put the gun away but the guy was really mad because Professor Bosco said something about him doing something with his mother. The man's mother. Not Professor Bosco's mother."

"I understand," I said, and motioned for her to continue.

"And then," she said, spreading her hands in a 'poof' gesture, "they were dead."

Elmira stared straight ahead, those infinitely deep blue eyes staring somewhere into another world.

Carmody cleared his throat and spoke gently.

"What exactly do you mean by, 'and then they were dead?'"

"Swingle," she said.

"What about Swingle?" I coaxed.

"Oh, he shot them all," Elmira said, distantly, with the same tone you'd use to say, "Oh, he mailed all the letters yesterday."

Bosco's voice filled the room as he stepped through the batwings. I hadn't heard him approach and I was angry at myself for letting my guard down. Relaxing after you think the shooting is over is how a lot of men wind up taking the eternal dirt nap.

Bosco knew what I was thinking and held up his spread hands, palm out, in apology.

And then he pointed to his feet.

"The one you call Swingle. He stood right here and started cutting them down, a pistol in his right hand and a rifle on his left hip. They started firing back and he just stood there, like he didn't care. I don't know how they missed, but they did. Guess he's a small target, but the son of a bitch just stood there and *smiled.*"

Elmira reached down, balled up the hem of her dress in one hand and used it to scrub the mouth of the bottle. She started to pour herself another shot but her hand was still shaking and she sank into her chair and muttered to *hell with it* and stuck the bottle in her mouth, holding it with both hands until she'd finished.

"They skedaddled after that," she said, setting the bottle down carefully, still maneuvering two-handed, her bright but unfocused eyes intent on making sure that the bottle made proper contact with the table. "Right through my office and out the back door. We'd all hit the floor but Swingle chased them right around the building to the front, where they were trying to get their horses."

"I was not in the war," Bosco, said, "I was overseas at the time, but I imagine what happened next is what war sounds like."

"Boom, boom, boom," Elmira said.

Then she nodded approval to herself. "Yep, boom, boom, boom, boom, boom, boom…"

Bosco interrupted.

"And by the time I peeled myself off the floor and looked out, those two other men ran round the corner, saying they were on our side. One was carrying a big rifle and the other a popgun or something, but the shooting was over. The little guy was already dragging the bodies around."

We were all silent for a moment.

"He's a lot stronger than he looks," Bosco concluded.

Chapter 16

I guided Elmira to her room so she could get a couple hours of sleep before Bosco's first show. Carmody and I borrowed a wagon pulled by two surly mules and loaded up the bodies. I gave up on my policy of holding the bodies for identification because I couldn't keep stacking them like cordwood. So we loaded them on the bed of the wagon, retrieved the ripening body from my office, and headed to the cemetery.

There's no undertaker in Shadow Valley. Ours had died shortly before I arrived and no members of that profession had since shown an interest in us, which surprised me because we certainly produced a reliable supply of new business.

By mutual agreement, Carmody dug the graves, a task for which he has an astonishing skill that was probably honed in wartime, although I've given up asking about it because he always deflects the questions.

This time he wanted to ask me a question.

"After such a period of rapid expansion," he said, "I christened this part the Josiah Hawke wing of the cemetery. But now that you've got your little buddy contributing, should I start in a new direction? Maybe call it the Snake Swingle – what's the word – *annex?"*

I didn't let myself get drawn in, and said nothing, and he didn't comment further. But he did, with some dramatic flair, pull back the blankets covering the faces of the bodies before we planted them, presumably to ensure they were routed to the Hawke wing or the Swingle annex.

"Got another question," Carmody said, scooping out rocky dirt with an effortless and relentless rhythm. "What are we gonna do about that crazy weasel?"

It was, at last, a legitimate question, so I didn't mind answering.

"He says he's going to stay locked up until we decide whether to charge him."

Swingle had voluntarily checked himself back into his cell after the conclusion of what locals were calling The Battle of Shadow Valley, adamant that he'd always been a good soldier and followed rules to the letter. I didn't want to have to baby-sit him so I let him keep the keys so he could orchestrate his own outhouse and meal breaks.

Carmody shrugged and shook his head.

"Guess you could make a case either way. I didn't see how the kerfuffle began, and witnesses gave me different versions of who had his gun out first. Not even sure that matters. Problem is, though, that if he gets off Scot-free there are going to be some who think you let him go because you owe him one."

"I owe him two, actually," I said.

"No question," Carmody said, "Elmira could have got roughed up, maybe worse, if Swingle hadn't waded in. Folks say when he tracked those goons to the street he didn't even blink when they opened up on him. He just stayed cool and put his shots where they counted."

I nodded.

"He's one of those people who don't feel fear," I said. "Literally, for him it doesn't exist. I don't know if he's crazy or if he was born missing the part of his brain that tells normal people not to walk into gunfire."

Carmody covered up the last body, patted down the earth with the back of his shovel, and spoke almost absently, finally asking the question he'd wanted to ask but was waiting for the time.

"He tells everybody who's willing to listen, and even those who ain't, that he saved your life, and you didn't call him a liar, so I guess it's true. But I never got the particulars."

I told Carmody that if I told him the story he'd call *me* a liar, but we had an hour before Bosco's show, and if he really wanted to hear, it was a story best told over another whiskey.

Chapter 17

S wingle had been traveling with my division when the Rebs had turned two deafening twelve-pound mountain howitzers on us, and our backs were against the wall, literally. We'd been driven back by the cannon fire all morning, and didn't know the geography. These were local Virginia mountain boys, and they knew that the valley closed in to a U-shape and our retreat would eventually back us into a steep rocky mountainside that would pen us in on three sides.

When I figured out what was happening it was too late. I tried riding to the side, looking for an escape, but my horse was shot out from beneath me and I was hit in the leg.

The howitzers were loaded with canister shot, and the Rebs weren't rationing their fire, so it looked like they had plenty more where that came from. The little howitzers didn't have the range of a big Napoleon gun, but at 500 yards or so could produce a murderous spread. Each of the 150 or so balls in a canister, each ball the size of an old-fashioned musket ball, could pulverize bone and body, and that's what happened to my horse. I think I was hit with shrapnel from the shell-shaped canister that held the balls, because I had a long, jagged cut across my leg instead of a puncture mark.

I crawled behind the dead horse and started firing from behind what cover he offered. There were riflemen along the flanks of the two pieces of artillery, and I took a few shots at them. The men operating the cannon were more vulnerable – they were working the wheels of the pieces, locomoting them forward, while one man loaded each piece and another fired. But cutting them down was futile because they'd be replaced in an instant. So I concentrated on the immediate threat to me – the Rebs turning their rifles in my direction.

You can't hear much of anything in a din like that, but I heard the yell.

It was the corporal they called Snake because he liked to hide and ambush the enemy and had a reputation for striking suddenly and without mercy. I'd never talked with him in the two days I'd been with the unit, and he wasn't under my direct command. But another lieutenant told me that the Snake was completely insane, which wasn't a bad attribute in battle, at least most of the time.

If you could judge from the crazy yell, the little man had his cuckoo clock permanently stuck on twelve. The sound coming out of him wasn't like the war whoops you hear from men on both sides, or from the Indians. It was like the earth had opened up and Satan himself had vented his demonic rage.

And as I hunkered behind a dead horse, my blood pooling beneath my useless leg, Confederate riflemen advancing on me, I did what any crack officer would do under the circumstances.

I lay there with my mouth hanging open and watched the crazy little son of a bitch charge the west-side cannon.

What happened next I can only chalk up to the fact that the canisters are packed with sawdust to separate the balls and make them spread. Without the spreading effect, the load would just punch a massive hole directly forward, instead of laying down a wide swath of anti-personnel fire. I suppose some mathematician could figure out the space between the spreading balls and compute it against the distance of the target and figure out how close you could get to the mouth of the cannon and still somehow slip between the flying lead. But theory aside, somehow the sinewy little lunatic did it.

He was no more than 30 yards from the mouth of the beast, and was unscathed.

It takes about twenty seconds for a crew to sponge, load, fuse and fire a howitzer, but it took Swingle about half that time to kill the corporal in charge of the weapon and unload his repeating rifle in the general direction of the rest of crew, who scattered like mice when the pantry door opens.

The riflemen on the flanks finally turned their attention to Swingle. I assumed that *they* had assumed he was a heartbeat away from death and ignored him, but now he had their full attention.

Swingle drew a Colt Dragoon, an absurdly big pistol to begin with. And it looked comically oversized in Swingle's hands.

But Swingle killed one of them with a single shot.

Three Rebs nearby pivoted toward Swingle and I stood up and cut them down with three shots, the speed and accuracy of which I could not now reproduce for a million dollars even if I had every hour of every day for the rest of my life to try.

Then my leg got the message that it wasn't supposed to work anymore and I toppled forward, now effectively shielding the dead horse with *my* body. I tried to prop myself on an elbow but things were getting gray; my field of vision had narrowed and I felt as though I were peering through twin smoky tunnels.

Before I blacked out the last thing I saw was Swingle turn the little howitzer 90 degrees, pull the wire on the friction fuse, and blast the other cannon and crew. The spokes on the wheels of the other howitzer flew apart like kindling and the crew were erased from the earth.

When I woke up they told me our troops had immediately advanced and laid down a hail of fire, and Swingle had somehow managed to reload and fire the howitzer by himself, blowing away a dozen Rebs and forcing the rest to back up.

Mind you, firing a cannon isn't like putting a bullet in a chamber and pulling the trigger. You have to wipe out the barrel pretty carefully or the thing is just as likely to explode and kill you instead of the enemy. Next you have to plunge in the powder and the shell, insert the canister or grape shot, and change fuses.

Then you pull the wire, which, on a friction fuse, grates against a small explosive in the fuse and sets off the powder in the chamber.

Somehow, with bullets swarming around him like mosquitoes, Swingle figured out how to do all that.

Union troops overran the position and took over crewing the canons. Even though the wheels and the trail had been shattered on the unit Swingle blasted, the cannon itself survived. It only weighs a little over 200 pounds, so a crew can move the thing by hand. If you can find a big rock to brace it against its own recoil and a log to elevate the barrel, it still does its deadly job.

The battle turned into a rout, I was told. Union casualties were light. I'd been lucky to survive – not entirely because of my wound, which was jagged and bled a lot but was superficial – but because I'd been dragged off the field soon after being hit.

I'm not an extraordinarily big man, a little over six feet and about the same weight as the barrel of the howitzer, but it did take an extraordinary effort to get me out of the line of fire, the field surgeon told me.

The little corporal did it by himself, the surgeon said, after an experienced cannon crew had taken over his cannon and the little fellow had nothing else to do.

Chapter 18

Sheeeee-it, Carmody said after I'd finished the story. He could drag the word out and modulate it throughout an entire octave, like a profane opera singer.

"That just about says it all," I said. "I don't know for sure if he saved my life or not, no one could tell that for certain, but you can see why I can't stick him in a cell or run him out of town."

"And he just showed up out of nowhere, two weeks ago? Not looking for you?"

"He says no, and unless he's a better actor than I give him credit for, he seemed surprised to see me. Marched in my office, said he was bounty hunting, looking for some rustlers, and wanted to check with me about some local brands he'd never seen before."

Carmody looked at himself in the mirror behind the bar. I'd promised Elmira I'd paint the thing. The glass was halfway decent but the frame had rotted and turned a rusty gray, the color I associated with decaying rodents.

"Man like that could prove useful someday," he said.

"The next time we feel the need to stage a massacre," I said, "he'll be indispensable."

Then I looked at myself in the mirror behind the bar. I didn't entirely like what I saw. My hair was getting gray on the sides, not a silver gray that might somehow make me look like a senator or something, but the dull gray that you'd associate with an old metal tool. The vertical furrows on the side of my mouth seemed deeper than I remembered, my eyebrows bushier, and my general demeanor meaner.

It was probably the light. I checked and Carmody didn't look that good, either.

In the reflection I saw Elmira glide in, and she somehow looked wonderful, even in the uncharitable lighting. She'd enjoyed a couple hours of deep sleep, induced, no doubt, by half a bottle of whiskey, and she'd changed into a black gown that set off the metallic gold and silver of her hair.

I'd always thought of her in metallurgical terms. She had some wrinkles, for sure, but not the claw marks that are ravaged into the faces of so many women of her age and occupation. Her wrinkles looked more like the fine lines stamped delicately on the face of a gold coin.

"We should get over there," she said. "We need to get our seats in the fourth row center."

Carmody groaned.

Elmira had heard that fourth row center were the best seats in the house and insisted we plunk ourselves there, even though the pew-style seating

was punishingly tight and Carmody, with his absurdly long limbs, looked like pile of tent-poles
jammed between the rows at odd and random angles.

"Maybe I should stay here and keep order,"
he said.

"Come on, you'll love the show," she said.
"I've seen his reviews, and his tricks are amazing."

Carmody tilted his head forward.

"I'm no dummy," he said. "I'm a law enforcement officer trained to notice things. You think
I'm going to be all mystified because he palms a
card or puts a false bottom hat over a trap-door table
and pulls out a rabbit?"

"Please?" Elmira said.

Carmody sighed and downed the last of his
drink and marched off toward two hours of squirming in his seat and jamming his elbow into my ribs.

The man is made entirely of pointy angles and
he insists on sitting almost on top of me.

"Don't expect me to fall for that stuff," he
said, and tugged the brim of his hat down harder
than he needed to.

Chapter 19

Sheeee-it, Carmody said as we sat with Bosco in a corner table after the show.

"How in *hell did you do that*?" Carmody said, and shook his head.

Bosco was going to say something but was interrupted by a granite-faced cowhand who'd planted himself in front of us, one of those dour and forbidding men who makes you wonder if he'd ever laughed, even as a kid, or if he'd scowled with menace while he was ten years old, jumping into a swimming hole or catching frogs.

"How in hell did you do that?" the cowhand said. And then he stuck out his hand and told Bosco it was the greatest show he'd ever seen and clapped him on the shoulder and somberly turned his back and walked away.

It had been like that in the hour since the show ended. Dozens of well-wishers had gushed over Bosco, and Bosco unfailingly stood ramrod-straight for the men as well as the women and said that he was merely a humble illusionist and that their enjoyment of the show made him genuinely happy, and then he would bow.

And when the spirit moved him, he'd kiss a woman's hand, holding it in his hand with his pinky extended. I wondered if that was a custom in Newark, but decided not to ask.

Elmira wasn't sitting with us. The bar was hopping, busier than I'd ever seen it, and she and the staff couldn't keep up. Nonie, a little mute girl I'd found wandering on horseback a year or so ago, was fetching empty bottles and glasses like she was in some sort of contest, and she was puffing like a blowing horse.

Her name really isn't Nonie, and I'd never been able to find out her real moniker, even though I'd investigated the incident that caused her parents' death, a massacre on the nearby rise we called the Mountain of Slow Madness. It had blasted her mind into a state of perpetual silence.

When we took her in, Elmira had started calling her "No Name," which I thought was a little harsh, so I shortened it.

When the last trickle of genuflectors had ended, I asked Bosco why he always insisted on pointing out that his tricks were just tricks.

His expression turned serious.

"You don't want anybody to get the idea that you're involved in 'magic,'" he said. "I'm serious. We're not that far from time when people who believed you somehow tapped into dark powers would burn you at the stake. The last thing I want is a nut who thinks I'm a warlock. You wouldn't believe how many crazy people there are in this world."

"I'd believe it," Carmody said.

"Damn straight," I said.

"However," Carmody said, "I firmly do not believe in black magic or witches or ghosts or goblins but I just don't get how the hell you did it any other way."

"We generally don't give away our tricks," Bosco said, "but you're both sworn officers and everybody says you're honest, so I'll make you a deal: I won't tell you how a trick is done. But if you figure it out yourself I'll tell you if you're right and buy you a drink. But you've got to promise that it stays at this table. From what I've heard you both have developed a reputation for unraveling mysteries, so give it a try."

We all shook on it.

"I know one answer and only one," Carmody said. "The girl who disappeared and reappeared in the back of the auditorium. Them girls is twins."

Bosco seemed startled and looked at me.

"I didn't tell him," I said.

Bosco leaned forward on his elbows.

"How could you tell?"

"Them low-cut dresses."

Bosco waited, unaware that Carmody would insist in being coaxed through this journey through incomprehensibility.

"All right," Bosco, relented, "what about the low-cut dresses?"

"One girl's got a mole on her bosom." He said it *boo-zum*. "The other one don't."

Bosco looked skeptical.

"Tom has incredible eyesight," I said. "And incredible powers of concentration, once something catches his interest."

"But the spell you cast on me," Carmody said, "was real. I couldn't lift it."

The "spell" was cast after Bosco asked the audience who the strongest man in the town was. Carmody didn't volunteer, but everyone turned to him out of reflex. Carmody was summoned on stage and asked if he could lift a box off the floor, which he could with ease. Next, little Nonie was called on stage, and asked if she could lift the box, which she did with a little effort. Then Bosco said he was putting a spell on Carmody to rob him of his power – and Carmody couldn't lift the box. He grunted, snarled, and his veins were bulging out on his arms and forehead, but he could not budge the box until Bosco released the spell.

Carmody was dumbfounded at the time, and remained so as he poured himself another drink.

"Theories?" Bosco asked me.

"There's an electromagnet under the stage," I said, "and the bottom of the box is lined with iron."

Bosco cut his eyes at me and I could read what he suspected.

"No, I didn't sneak into the theater and check," I said. But I can't think of any other reason why you would build a stage on top of a stage other than to hide something beneath it."

Bosco nodded noncommittally, still not fully buying my claim that I hadn't used my key and spied on the auditorium floor, which I had not.

"I know a little bit about the history of war," I said, "and unless I'm wrong this is the same trick a magician named Jean Eugène Robert-Houdin used in 1856 on behalf of the French who were fighting in Algeria."

Bosco smiled and shook his head slowly.

"You got me," he said. "Touché."

"Am I gonna be the house dummy all night," Carmody said, "or can somebody tell me what this is all about?"

"Houdin was the greatest of European magicians," Bosco said. "The French who occupied Algeria were having a devil of a time with warlords who convinced the natives that they exercised magical control. The French brought in Houdin and he did the 'light and heavy chest' trick to show everyone that the French were no slouches when it came to magic spells."

"So how's it work?" Carmody said.

"You remember the deal," Bosco said, and turned to me. He wasn't going to explain; the onus was on me.

"I'll do my best," I said, and turned to Carmody. "You make electricity with magnets and wires, like the electricity in the telegraph lines. A generator moves wires though a magnetic field to make power."

"I *know* that," Carmody said. "I ain't no dummy."

"But the point is that if you wrap wires with electricity going through them around metal, they turn the electricity back to magnetism. An electromagnet. And unless I miss my bet, there's an electromagnet under the stage hooked up to a big lead-acid battery that Bosco had charged up in advance. His assistants flipped a switch somewhere when it came your turn to lift it and he cast his 'spell.'"

Bosco leaned forward and spoke in a near-whisper.

"I trust you'll keep that to yourselves," he said. "And I might add, if it makes you feel better, Mr. Carmody, that I ended the trick early because I could see you'd pried one corner off the floor and you were either going to break the magnetic field and lift it or break the box trying. Or maybe actually tear up the floor. No one's come close to doing that in the ten years I've been performing the illusion. You probably were exerting about five hundred pounds of force."

"I can carry a five hundred pound hog under one arm," Carmody said, pouting.

"Maybe you were even lifting six or seven hundred pounds," Bosco said.

"Never head a such a thing as an electromagnet," Carmody said.

"Electricity is all the rage nowadays," Bosco said. "This year they put electric street lights in Paris."

"Ain't nobody going to pick them up and steal them," Carmody said.

Bosco cleared his throat and changed the subject.

"That's one drink I owe both of you. Tell me how I read minds and I'll make it a bottle each."

Bosco had closed the show with a mind-reading act, and received a standing ovation.

Gina – or maybe it was Louisa, I'm not as astute a student of *boo-zums* as Carmody – sat blindfolded on stage, facing away from the audience, and guessed what objects audience members had shown to Bosco, holding the article in their laps so even most of the audience couldn't see what they possessed. Bosco would ask questions – what is it, what is it made of, what color is it? After Gina had identified the object – eyeglasses, metal, gold in color, for example – the astonished audience member would hold it aloft.

Carmody knitted his brows together and put his chin on his fists.

"In fact," Bosco said, "if you guess this one, I'll make it a case."

'A case for both of us?" Carmody said.

"A case for *each* of you."

I could almost hear the wheels and gears grinding inside Carmody's head.

"You was talking in a code," Carmody said.

"Go on," Bosco said. "Prove it."

"You'd start by saying stuff nobody would pay no notice to, like, 'I'm holding in my hand,' or

'I have here," or "I'm looking at,'" Carmody said. "I think you've got ten or twenty phrases like that – meaningless things you start out with – and they each let Gina know what category the object is. Eyeglasses, or a pen. 'I have here' might mean it's a pen."

"You're sure it was Gina?" I asked.

Carmody winked and pointed to his left eye.

"I has unusual powers of observation, too."

"Go on," Bosco urged.

"Stuff that's in people's pockets," Carmody said, "is already narrowed down a mite. You ain't going to find a kangaroo or a piano. Almost every-thing would fall into categories like eyeglasses, pens, knives, derringers, compasses, magnifying glasses, handkerchiefs. If somebody did have a kan-garoo, you just wouldn't have picked him in the first place from the people in the audience holding out their stuff for you to see."

Bosco nodded, staying non-committal and cagey. He wasn't about to confirm or deny anything Carmody had posited. Carmody seemed right on the beam so far. Carmody is not one to be up-to-date on electricity and streetlights, but subterfuge and codes are right up his alley.

Carmody stuck that tree-branch finger straight up and wagged it, getting into the spirit of his lec-ture.

"The next thing you'd do is ask Gina a ques-tion about what the thing was made of but you'd tell her in code. You'd always begin the question with some stiff line like, 'pray tell,' or 'perchance you would be good enough.' Nobody talks like that."

"Not even in Newark," I said, noting as I spoke the words that I'd been drinking a little too quickly.

Bosco still looked unperturbed.

Carmody stabbed that horrid finger into the tabletop in a victory gesture.

"So those little saying would give it away. You'd say, 'pray tell,' and it might mean the color blue."

Bosco leaned in, suddenly.

"You're certainly not the only one who suspected something like that," he said. "And you remember that for the last four objects I proved that I wasn't code-talking by drinking from a glass of water when the audience member held the object."

Carmody was deflated.

Bosco was elated.

But not for long. I had the answer.

"You were using a code based on *time*," I said.

Bosco's expression grew stony.

"You kept the glass with you and set in on the floor after you drank from it." I said. "You'd start by saying, 'look at the object while I drink from this glass' each time. And you set it down pretty hard. I think you and Gina were counting each second in your head. One second was one category, two seconds was another, and so on. You'd end the count when you set the glass down on the wood."

Bosco said nothing and I knew I had him.

"And each of the last four items were simple objects you could guess with one code. The last one was a silver knife. The handle wasn't silver but you grabbed it and held it up and took the blade out first before you held it up. All blades are silver color. So I'll bet 'silver' was something like a seven-second count."

Bosco sighed and looked straight ahead, focusing on nothing in particular.

"How did you figure that out?"

"Mister," Carmody said, "You don't know who you're dealing with here. Josiah is a human bag of tricks. During the war he stuck logs into the ground and made the enemy think they was cannons. He marched men through a clearing in a circle, twenty men going in a circle for hours and the Reb scouts watching from the next hill over thought it was a division. You is two of a kind. You ought to join up and do an act."

"I'm not sure I'd be much of a showman," I said, noticing that the words were coming out with some difficulty. I needed to slow down my drinking a little. But it had been a tense day.

"Showman? You're the best piano-playing gunfighter in the world," Carmody said.

"I'll bet those words have never been spoken in that order in the history of the English language," Bosco said, and I noted that he was starting to slur his words a little, too.

"You know, Bosco," I said, "maybe we could switch roles, because I think you might make a good lawman. If you can figure out that code-talking you can probably put things together in your head in ways most people can't. Maybe you can solve a mystery instead of creating one. I've got one on my hands right now."

He raised his eyebrows to show me he was game.

"If you help me," I said, "I'll forgive you your debt."

'We get whiskey for free here anyway," Carmody said.

"You shouldn't have told him that," I said.

"What mystery is you talking about?" Carmody said.

"Sorry, Tom, I've been so busy with the Battle of Shadow Valley that I didn't have a chance to tell you."

They both looked at me.

I let them wait, building a little suspense. Despite what I told them, I *am* a pretty good showman.

"This morning," I said, "I got a letter from a dead man."

Chapter 20

We waited until the next morning to get serious about the Marner business. I'd tried explaining the dead man's letter the night before but didn't have it with me and forgot the highlights, and my lips went numb, and Bosco's chin kept slipping off his palm as he tried to pay attention.

We met in Elmira's office because Swingle was still a guest of the town, having taken up residence at what he called his "luxury iron bar hotel." I've never met a man who liked a cell so much.

I let him keep the keys and he came and went as he pleased. As some madmen tend to be, he was obsessively neat. He was sweeping a corner of the room near the safe when I stopped in to retrieve Marner's letter before I met with Carmody and Bosco.

I have to admit, I was impressed. At some point in the morning, he'd even rearranged the wanted posters I'd haphazardly tacked up on the wall and they were now lined up as neatly as a display in an art gallery.

It occurred to me, and in fact startled me, when I remembered that I'd not locked up the guns yesterday when I'd gone to confront the men coming down the trail, and the only place Swingle could have grabbed all that firepower was from my little arsenal. Swingle's gun was still in the safe.

Now the rifles and two handguns were lined up neatly as soldiers and the chain re-looped through the trigger guards and secured with the fussy padlock. Everything was gleaming. The crazy little weasel had even oiled up and polished the barrels.

Swingle asked me if I'd decided whether or not to charge him yet and I said I hadn't made up my mind and that seemed to suit him just fine. I told him there was some petty cash in the top drawer of my desk and he could buy himself breakfast.

He said he'd get to it once he cleaned the glass in the front window.

I should incarcerate him in the Spoon, I thought as I entered through the back door. The place stunk. The blended aroma of spilled beer, puke, and smoke is particularly insulting to the senses at nine in the morning. Everything, in fact, seemed out of order. The brilliant shaft of light angling in through the window, illuminating a cloud of swirling dust mites, seemed astonishingly out of place.

Bosco looked like I felt, and was massaging his temples. Carmody never gets hangovers and was in one of his cheerful moods, a habit that in early mornings makes me doubt the wisdom of me being armed in his presence.

"Extra strong," he said, handing me the coffee he'd just brewed, his unique formula that somehow tastes like it's already made a first pass through the kidneys.

I read Marner's letter out loud and followed up with the article.

Bosco was beginning to revive and took a sip from the battered tin cup. Then he raised an eyebrow and looked down into the center of the cup, regarding it with some suspicion.

"What is this?" Bosco said.

"It's coffee," Camody said.

"Really?"

Bosco shrugged and took another swallow and then asked if he could see the letter. He held it up to the slanting sunlight.

"Looks real," he said.

Carmody stepped over near the window and asked Bosco what he meant.

"I mean that the way it's written indicates a man under great stress," Bosco said. "I'm not sure why anyone would fake a letter asking for help, but it could happen and I can't speak to the facts of the situation. But the writer believed that there was danger and he was angry and confused."

Carmody raised one eyebrow, impressively high and with great theatrical flair. I believe he must practice that expression in a mirror.

"It's not really a trick," Bosco said, "but something I've studied. I used to use it as part of a mind-reading act. I'd turn my back and ask somebody to write me a letter and then I'd identify who it was. It's not as hard as you might think, because if the audience is half men and half women it's easy to identify writing by sex and you can cut the number of potential writers in half from the beginning. Then, if the writing is left-handed, you look around the room to see who's wearing a sidearm on the left-hand side. Or if someone is expensively dressed you assume he's educated and you identify him with good spelling and the formation of letters. And just for good measure I'd supply the pen and paper and the pen would be leaky and I could sometimes spot a smudge of ink on the writer's hand."

"You don't do that trick anymore?" I asked.

"It's like card tricks. They work in small groups but not so well for large audiences. Besides, with more people to choose from the odds of getting the handwriting identification wrong are higher, anyway. I used to work small audiences, doing parlor tricks, but now I'm a victim of my own success."

I joined Bosco and Carmody by the window and asked Bosco to get back to Marner.

"Look at the slant of the letters," Bosco said. "In addition to the whole line slanting down, showing he's not optimistic, sometimes the letters tilt left and sometimes they tilt right. That shows confusion and an agitated emotional state. The letter is written with a great deal of pressure on the pen and the dots on the letter *I* are more like slashes. That indicates anger. But still, it's carefully written, the sign of a man under great stress who is acting with great deliberation, perhaps knowing that a great deal is at stake. Perhaps his life."

"Golly," Carmody said, his eyes alight with childlike wonder. "You're pretty good."

Bosco didn't bow, exactly, but bobbed his head.

I had no idea whether Bosco's deductions emerged from science or from the south end of a north-facing horse, but he made sense. I reminded myself that convincing people that improbable things made sense was Bosco's business, and he was good at it, so I reserved some skepticism.

Still, he was good at what he did, very good, as skilled as Carmody was with a rifle and as proficient as I was with my fists.

So I took a gamble.

"Are you interested in a side job?" I said.

Chapter 21

Bosco had one more show in Shadow Valley, and then a week off before he started an engagement in Austin. I had a pretty good pot of town money available to hire a special deputy. Bosco took on the assignment.

I wanted him to ride to New Paradise and nose around concerning the death of Gus Marner. Carmody or I couldn't leave town, not in the aftermath of an as-yet unexplained attack. We had no idea what was to come, and for all I knew the Marner letter could be a ruse to lure me away from town.

Bosco had the perfect cover, he told me, warming to the idea as though he were planning a stage trick. It wasn't unusual for illusionists, he told me, or any kind of itinerant performer, to make cold sales calls in towns they were traveling through, and a gambling hall would be the logical first stop. He'd bring Gina along, stashing her out of sight in his wagon until he got out of town, giving her a reprieve to alternately hiding out with Louisa. And with Gina away, Louisa could move freely around town, escaping her isolation, too, without fear of bumping into herself and giving away their secret.

Carmody reconnoitered with Bosco over a map and figured it to be a seven-hour trip in the wagon, and Bosco said he'd leave before dawn and aim to return after sundown the following day.

Bosco told me had had to go back to the auditorium and fix a few things before tonight's show, including the Carmody-damaged box with the steel bottom.

I told Bosco that would be fine because I had to wait out front and sign for some liquor, which we expected this morning. Elmira had a load coming in from a supplier in Austin, and none too soon: Bosco drew a crowd that liked to tip a few while meeting him at the bar after the show, and as a result we were running low on whiskey.

It was only 10:30, too early to open, and at least an hour before Elmira would pry herself out of bed, but I unlocked and opened the doors in back of the batwings. The place could use an airing-out, I decided and I busied myself by sweeping the floor, and because it was getting breezy, sweeping it again after the dust blew back in from the street.

An hour later I had swept pretty much every molecule of dirt from the place and was getting annoyed and more than a little worried. The delivery was late, and if it didn't show by tonight we might run out and have to close early. That's not the worst thing in the world – Elmira has an informal agreement with the owner of the other place in town, Eddie Moon, that in such circumstances we will herd people to his bar, the eponymous Full Moon, if he returns the favor. We've traded clientele four or five times in the past year when one or the other place ran low on beer or liquor, or closed after being busted up in a fight.

I thought about tracking down Carmody and asking him to wait for the liquor wagon but I didn't have anything pressing so I figured I'd polish glasses for a while.

And then it dawned on me that Swingle had considerable time on his hands and he might as well wait here in the bar as in his beloved cell. I was about to fetch him when I smelled the wagon as soon as I heard it.

The breeze carried the smell of a mixture of whiskey, gin, and beer, an olfactory concoction that really turns your stomach before noon when you are nursing a hangover.

I wondered if the wholesaler had a cork shortage or something and walked out the front and saw the driver.

He recognized me, held out a hand, tried to talk through a bloody mouthful of broken teeth, and fell into the pile of dust I'd just swept onto Front Street.

Chapter 22

There's a doctor who makes a circuit to town every week or so but in his absence we leave nursing duties to Dorothea Dwinn, otherwise known around town as the Widow Dwinn, who is Carmody's sometime girlfriend.

Dorothea had been a nurse on troop and passenger trains during the war and knew her way around bumps and bruises, of which this guy had plenty. He'd been worked over, he told us when he fully came around, by three men who had waylaid him about five miles out of town and had methodically taken clubs to him and the stock in the back of the delivery wagon until everything, including him, was pretty much pulverized.

They'd told him that should be ashamed of himself for wholesaling such crappy liquor and that they had taken it on themselves to stanch the flow or such rotgut. They added a strong suggestion that he change suppliers and said that it was likely someone would be contacting him.

Dorothea said he'd be all right and wiped her enormous hands on a bar rag. She bore an uncanny resemblance to Carmody: She was close to six feet tall and seemed to be entirely constructed of knees and elbows. Dorothea also emanated some of Carmody's affable menace. While she was a guffawing backslapper most of the time, rumor had it that her widow status was self-imposed after she'd caught the former Mr. Dwinn in some extracurricular activities and remedied the situation, permanently, with a fireplace poker.

But all that was long before my time and none of my business.

Right now, my business consisted of checking the battered wholesaler, whose name was Backus – although it might have been Baxter because he was hard to understand with his face all swollen up like that – into the hotel for the night.

Normally I'd let someone recuperating from a beating stretch out in an unlocked cell, but Swingle had staked out his territory indefinitely. Today he was using a wire brush to scale the rust off the bars. I paid for the hotel out of my own pocket. I sensed that Backus' beating had something to do with me, though I couldn't imagine how, and felt badly about it.

I wanted to sound Carmody about it but he and Dorothea were spending the afternoon doing chores at her small ranch. A few months ago, some hard cases who'd tried to lure Carmody into a trap had burned her house down.

But the thugs were dead now, and the new house, which Carmody had rebuilt with help from everyone in town who was afraid to say no to him, meaning everybody, was almost finished and it was a vast improvement on the original.

Sometimes things work out.

I wanted to see what Elmira thought about Backus' beating, but she was still asleep, and trying to extract any sense out of her before she came to was pointless. She had a unique talent whereby she could pretend to hear and mumble vague responses but remain asleep and have no recollection whatsoever of my futile attempt at contact. It was like holding a séance with a taciturn ghost.

So I cleaned up the wagon as best I could without cutting myself to shreds on the remains of the bottles, stabled Backus' horses, and decided I would pay a visit to Eddie Moon.

Moon is a congenial cutthroat. When I first came to Shadow Valley he was my prime suspect in a plot to put Elmira out of business, but while he was involved in the affair, his strings were being pulled by some powerful interests who wanted to drive Elmira out of business so they could buy up her property.

The bar and bordello, it turned out, were secondary. It was the scrubland she owned in back that was the jackpot because some connected interests had learned that there was a railroad planned to cut right through it.

The goon who pressured Moon was Purcell, the man who killed my predecessor. In my haste to kill Purcell, who was in a similar hurry to dispose of me, I'd neglected to determine whether Purcell hatched the plot on his own or if there was a bigger spider at the center of the web.

In the end, it didn't matter. The train project was as dead as Purcell. I'd heard through my own sources that grafters with bigger pockets had gotten the plans redrawn.

Moon, I, and Elmira never became what you'd call buddies. But even though I suspect that if it served his purpose he'd figuratively cut our throats in a second, my world is largely populated by people who would do that literally, so Elmira and I peacefully coexisted with him. Occasionally, like today, I'd do him a favor by buying up – at a handsome but expected markup – any excess liquor stock he had warehoused. If he didn't have any extra with which to gouge me, I'd close up early and send him our dispossessed clientele.

The Full Moon was open and the bartender was sweeping. After a hot summer and the dry days of early autumn, dust becomes the primary element of life around here, and we spend an inordinate amount of time moving it from one place to another.

In addition to getting cheated on the liquor supply, I also planned to see if Moon could offer some insight into what was happening.

Moon worked with a different liquor wholesaler, but if there was some sort of shakedown going on he might have caught wind of it.

I didn't suspect that Moon had anything to do with the goons who had trashed the Spoon, but I hadn't gotten around to asking him, so that would be on my agenda, too. Maybe he'd heard something that might be of use.

And I didn't know if Moon knew Gus Marner or had been to New Paradise, but I hadn't asked him about that either.

Guess I'm slowing down.

I confirmed that notion when I caught a glimpse of myself in the mirror behind Moon's bar. The sides of my head looked even grayer than back in the Spoon, where we had smaller windows and charitably darker environs.

The bartender looked up from his broom duty but didn't stop his machine-like scratching at the dust mites. He told me he hadn't seen Moon yet but this time of the morning Moon was usually in his back office.

I nodded and walked past the corner of the bar. The bartender looked like he wanted to tell me to wait while he fetched Moon, but gray hair or not I can still scowl with the best of them and he thought better of it and looked back down at the floor.

Moon's office was at the end of a narrow hallway that ran past his stockroom. I took a quick look in the stockroom – he'd do the same to Elmira, I'm sure – to assess the state of his inventory to gauge how badly I'd allow him to screw me if I made an offer to buy up his excess.

But I noticed that he wasn't exactly drowning in the stuff, either.

His office door was ajar so I walked right in. I knew it was rude, but I wanted to catch him by surprise.

When you're negotiating, it always helps to start with the other person off-balance.

But Moon was in no position to cut a deal.

He was slumped back in his green leather chair with a nickel-plated revolver in his hand and a bullet hole in his forehead.

Chapter 23

Carmody, Elmira, Bosco, and I sat in front of Moon's desk.

I'd sent the bartender to fetch Carmody right away but didn't provide any details, including the fact that Moon was dead. The barkeep was itching to ask what I was up to but I scowled at him again and he slunk away, glancing over his shoulder once, but deciding not to press me.

Apparently Carmody had interpreted my relayed message as an invitation to a social event because he brought two tag-alongs. It wasn't his fault; I'd been deliberately vague because I didn't want word to leak out just yet, but I couldn't tender the invitation myself because I didn't want to leave the scene unattended.

Elmira had let out a sharp, involuntary gasp when she entered the room and saw Moon, and her face immediately drained of color and became ashen slate. But as much as she recoils from violence, she can pull herself together when she knows it's important to keep her head, and she tottered to a desk chair and lowered herself carefully, as though she might break if she moved too quickly.

Bosco barely blinked. The experienced showman seemed to have nerves of steel – or the ability to pretend he had nerves of steel. Come to think of it, I'm not sure there is a difference.

Carmody took in the scene wordlessly and circled Moon's desk. He looked for an exit wound in the back of his Moon's head, there was none, which was consistent with the small-caliber popgun in Moon's hand. Little bullets go in and bounce around and can actually scramble the insides of a skull more than a big-bore through-and-through shot. Carmody then left the way he came in. I knew without asking that he'd scan the immediate area and the rooftops to assess whether there was a remaining threat. It was apparent to both of us that Moon had been dead for at least a few hours so an immediate danger was not likely.

But you never take chances in situations where guns and dead men are concerned. That's sort of our official motto, and it's kept me and Carmody most improbably alive long enough for my hair to start to turn what was the current color of Elmira's cheeks.

When Carmody came back, he shook his head in the all-clear sign and spoke for the first time.

"Sorry I took so long getting here," he said. "I was at Dorothea's…"

He searched for a word.

"*Helping.* I needed – well, she needed help with…"

I interrupted before Carmody felt the need, as he often does, of confessing to "succumbing to carnal desires" during working hours. That's how he chooses to express it – *succumbing to carnal desires* – and I urgently wanted to change the subject before it got to that point.

"Anything outside that might tell us something?" I said.

Reluctantly, as I'd interrupted his confessional, he got back to the business at hand.

"Hard to tell. There could be footprints outside the window, but with the wind and all this dust about it could just be smudges in the dirt. There's recent tracks in the road, lots of them, but nothing you wouldn't expect this time of day."

I noticed that Elmira had become alarmingly pallid, so I sat down next to her and held her hand, which was about as cold as I expected Moon's would be.

"He looks so...peaceful," she said.

"That's 'cause he's *dead,*" Carmody said, apparently for lack of anything better to say, although I was sure he could have come up with something better than that. He scraped a chair close to Elmira and held her other hand.

Bosco still looked a little hung over and didn't want to be the last man standing so he fetched another office chair, carried it to the desk and dropped down heavily into it.

We sat there, grouped around the desk, for a good thirty seconds, until it sunk in.

"It looks like we're holding a really, really strange meeting," Bosco said.

Elmira drew a ragged breath and forced a sickly smile.

"I half expect him to explain why he called us all here," she said.

We all knew it was no laughing matter so of course we started laughing.

Elmira straightened in her chair and told us that our behavior was completely inappropriate.

And then, of course, we all laughed harder.

Chapter 24

A few minutes later, Elmira gave one last ill-disguised giggle, took a few deep breaths, touched her hair as if to make sure it was still there, pasted on an all-business expression, and then asked no one in particular why Eddie Moon would shoot himself.

"If he *did* do it hisself," Carmody said.

Bosco asked if Carmody suspected otherwise.

"The only one who can tell us that for sure is Eddie Moon," Carmody said.

Bosco gave that half-chuckle again and asked Carmody if we were going to hold a séance.

"Josiah knows how to make the dead speak to him," Carmody said.

"I'm the last one who can speak for them," I said. Bosco merely nodded.

I think he caught Carmody's meaning. This was a man who didn't need things explained to him.

I pried the small revolver from Moon's hand, sniffed the barrel, and then sniffed the front and back of Moon's hand.

"I can still smell a strong odor of soot in the barrel," I said. "Which means that it's been fired in the last twelve hours or so. I can smell the burnt powder on Moon's hand, too. But the odor is stronger on the palm than on the back of the hand."

"Meaning?' Bosco said.

"Maybe nothing," I said, "but when you fire a gun the blowback hits the back of your hand and wrist and some of the powder blows out in back of the cylinder. The smell pretty much gets all over the gun and stays there for a few hours."

I handed Bosco the revolver.

"Grab it like you'd normally hold a gun," I said.

He did. He re-set his grip a couple times, un-comfortable, not knowing precisely what part of his hand went where.

"Smell the gun," I said.

He ran his nose the length of it like a hunting dog looking for tracks.

"Musty," he said. "Like burnt sulfur."

"It is sulfur," I said. "Mostly sulfur and char-coal. Now smell your hand, the front and back."

Bosco reversed his hand three times, nodded, and told me he could smell the burnt power on his palms and fingertips but nowhere else.

"You think the gun was placed in his hand af-ter it was fired?" he said.

"It's possible," I said, "but I can't be sure. Af-ter all, we're not bloodhounds and maybe this gun blows back differently from others I'm familiar with."

"But can someone even hold onto a gun after he kills himself?" Elmira said. "Wouldn't it fly out of his hand?"

Carmody held up that absurdly long finger, his signal that he wanted the floor.

"I got a theory on that. Depends on what part of your brain gets scrambled. I seen men killed from head wounds whose hands clutched up like bear traps. But sometimes they go limp. So it can happen either way."

"Fifty-fifty," I said.

"About that," Carmody concurred.

Bosco leaned forward.

"So it's plausible that he *did* shoot himself and kept the gun in his hand."

"I don't know yet," I said.

Elmira swallowed a couple of times, apparently in an effort to keep her digestive tract moving in the right direction, and said that if Moon had shot himself during the daylight morning hours, when some people in town were out and about, somebody surely would have heard it.

I told her that was a reasonable point and lifted Moon's arm a little and moved his head from side to side and she began to go gray again.

"He's too stiff for this to have happened this morning. I'm guessing middle of the night. Gun goes off in the middle of the night and most people sleep through it. And if they don't, they don't know what it was and go back to bed."

I put my palm under his chin and held Moon's head level and facing forward.

"What do you see in his hair?" I asked of no one in particular.

"The dust," Carmody said, with a certain air of finality, as though it settled everything, which maybe it did.

"What about the dust?" Elmira said.

Bosco came to his feet and touched the side of Moon's head.

"That clay dust from the street," he said, rubbing it between his thumb and fingers. "It's been so dry the last couple of weeks the dirt and dust gets tracked in everywhere."

Bosco reached down and drew a finger across the toe of his boot, revealing a streak of gleaming leather from under the yellowish powder. He did the same on the floor, exposing a stripe of burnished hardwood.

"He doesn't look like the type of man who would roll around on the floor for fun," Bosco said.

Carmody again circled the desk and began fussing with Moon's clothes. The dead man was dressed in a broadcloth blue shirt, a string tie, and a striped jacket.

"Known him for a year or so," Carmody said, "and I believe you're right. I also think he ain't the type to walk around with a split in the back seam of his jacket. Even I get mine sewn up when I split it there, which happens pretty much every time I get into a fight."

Elmira was looking queasy but I could tell she was intrigued.

"But he doesn't look like he's been fighting," she said. "I don't see any bruises."

Having spent a few years on the bareknuckle circuit, I'm an expert on bruises.

"Let's assume that somebody wanted to stage his death and make it look like a suicide," I said, "which is still just supposition, and I'm not even sure why anyone would want to do that. But in any event, *if* that were the plan, the last thing they'd want to do is leave traces of a beating."

I ran my hand through Moon's thick hair, which he wore long and backswept. Then I beckoned Bosco to do the same and asked him what he noticed.

Bosco felt with one hand, felt his own head, and then put a hand on both sides of Moon's head and probed with his fingertips.

"The right side is swollen. Maybe from the bullet?"

Carmody fingered the same spot and shook his head.

"This is goose-egg," Carmody said. "A swelling on top of the bone, not from underneath. I can tell because it moves around when I push it. A big egg just where you'd expect it if somebody who knew what he was doing laid Moon out with a sap."

"What's a sap?" Elmira said.

"A flat pouch of leather filled with lead shot," I said. "It looks like a beaver tail. People in certain businesses favor them because they don't leave much of a mark and usually don't break the skin and cause bleeding."

Elmira looked like she wanted to ask what business I was talking about but she'd gone from pale gray to sort of a frog-green and I could tell that her top priority was getting the hell out of that room, and I can't say I blamed her.

I was about to help her to her feet when Bosco spoke up in that commanding, cultured, contrived baritone. I'd have to ask him someday to say something in his original Newark voice.

"I know this is not my concern," he said, "but starting tomorrow I will be acting as a deputy."

Elmira flashed me a look of surprise that I found a little surprising in its intensity. I'd forgotten to tell her that I was sending Bosco to New Paradise in the morning. When I forget to tell her something, or just don't have the opportunity, she takes it as evidence I'm hiding something, even if there is no conceivable reason why I'd want to do so.

"I'll explain later," I said.

"And I'm sure you're aware that there are parallels between what might have happened there and what happened here, so I'm just trying to get some idea of what I'm walking into."

"All I know about what happened in New Paradise," I said, "is what I read in the newspaper article. Nothing more. I've never even been there."

"I have," Carmody said. "It's a shithole."

"But as far as Eddie Moon goes," I said, "I know he didn't shoot himself."

"How?" Bosco demanded.

I reached into Moon's center drawer, rummaging for a pen or pencil. I found one, a festive slate pencil with blue and white stars near the top and red and white stripes circling the lower half.

Elmira gasped and put her hand to her mouth as I stuck the pencil point into the hole in Eddie Moon's forehead.

Chapter 25

Bosco picked up on my thought process and peered into the center drawer and snatched a ledger book. He flipped through a couple pages.

"Assuming this is Eddie Moon's writing," he said, "he's right-handed."

"*Was* right-handed," Carmody said.

"Josiah," Elmira said in the soft and measured voice she employs at the Spoon when talking to a potentially violent drunk, "why are you sticking pencils in Eddie's head?"

Camody took a handful of Moon's hair and held the head upright, facing forward. The festive pencil protruded a few degrees to the right as we faced the body. In other words, to Moon's left.

"It shows the angle the shot went in," I said.

Carmody had to pull pretty hard to get the body into a fully upright position and the tension on the scalp pulled back the face a bit and Moon now appeared wide-eyed and smiling. It was a particularly ghastly complement to the festive pencil sticking out of a neat, charred hole in the center of his forehead.

"Oh, God," Elmira groaned, and put her elbows on the desk and laid her head down.

I figured she was better off like that than walking around so I picked up Moon's revolver and broke it open, pouring the rounds into my palm.

Only one had been fired.

"Do you know much about guns?" I asked Bosco.

"Not much at all."

"I do," I said, "and so does Tom, and we can assure you that I just completely unloaded the gun." I held it up to the window.

"You can see through the cylinder," I said. "That's where the bullets were and now all the chambers are empty. You can see through the barrel, and there's no bullet in there. There's nowhere for a bullet to hide."

"I understand," Bosco said, "but I don't know where you're going with this."

I turned to Carmody and asked him to help me move Moon's body out of the chair. Carmody is not allergic to showing a little swagger from time to time, and before I could get to Moon, Carmody put his arm under Moon's knees and scooped him up like a baby.

Moon wasn't a particularly big man but wasn't inconsiderable, either. I imagine he was about five-foot-ten and a hundred eighty pounds and Carmody stood there casually, holding him like a bag of apples, until I relented and said it would be all right to set him down now, so Carmody arranged the body in another chair. He fussed with the position of the head and demurely crossed Moon's hands in his lap.

Then I closed the revolver up, asked Bosco to sit in the desk chair, and handed him the piece.

"You never play around with a gun," I said to Bosco. "I don't know how many times I've mopped up after there's been an incident involving a gun that somebody thought was unloaded. That's why I made such a deal of unloading it and showing it to you and Carmody."

"Why?" Bosco said.

"Because now I want you to point it at your head and pull the trigger."

Bosco shrugged.

Elmira lifted her head, groaned again, and dropped it back on her forearms.

Chapter 26

I pointed the gun at the ground, pulled the trigger twice, and it clicked dry both times.

"This is a Smith and Wesson .22 caliber," I said. "It's named the Model 1 but most people call it a Smith and Wesson 'belly gun' because it's small and people tend to conceal them in their waistbands. A .22 is not a very powerful round. It wouldn't even penetrate the back of Moon's skull, but it works fine for close-up work. I know that Moon carried a gun – he actually kept it tucked in the back of his pants, and I saw him pull it once – but I don't remember if it was this one or not. But it's same general type of weapon."

I handed Bosco the pistol. He gripped it more comfortably this time, broke open the cylinder, spun it, and snapped it shut the way I had.

"Just point it anywhere and pull the trigger," I said.

Bosco aimed at the floor and clicked the action six times. He made a face as he did it.

"Not as easy as you'd suspect, is it?" I said. "I'd guess it has about an eight-pound trigger pull. Some guns are just sprung that way but I suspect

Moon's has a harder pull than normal because he didn't keep it oiled."

I then told Bosco to aim it at his head.

He pointed the barrel of the weapon upward toward his temple.

"That's the way a normal person would point a gun," I said. "But the bullet didn't go in upward through his temple. Look at the pencil."

We all turned to look at Moon's body and Carmody helpfully pointed toward the forehead in case somebody didn't get it.

"The bullet went into the forehead from an angle a little to the left and pointing a little down," Bosco said.

He turned the gun in his hand and put his thumb on the trigger.

"If I were going to shoot myself in the forehead, I'd do it like this."

I shook my head.

"But Moon didn't do it that way. When we found the body the gun was in a normal grip with his index finger on the trigger. Not his thumb."

Bosco assumed the earlier grip and raised the revolver. In order to get the right angle he had to crank his head to his right.

"No," I said. The head was blown straight back, not to the side. It was upright and facing straight forward when I came in."

Carmody spoke softly as he leaned in toward Bosco. Carmody held the muzzle between his thumb and forefinger and angled it toward Bosco's eyes.

"It ain't easy to look at, even when three of us know it ain't loaded," Carmody said, "I can't believe no one who's looking to shoot himself turns his face toward the place that's going to spit death in their face. They turn away and shoot into the temple, or keep the gun low where they can't see it and shoot through the roof of the mouth."

"So please hold your head forward and upright," I said, and Bosco complied.

"Now lift the gun near your hairline and point the barrel toward the center of your forehead."

Bosco strained to affect the position, cranking his wrist inward as far as he could.

"Pull the trigger," I said.

His wrist was bent so far that only the tip of his index finger could reach the trigger, and from that position he had no leverage.

"You're a strong man with big hands and tremendous physical dexterity," I said. "Can you pull the trigger from that position?"

"No," he said quietly, and set the gun gently on the desk.

"Can I look up now?" Elmira asked in a small, muffled voice, her face still planted in her arms.

Chapter 27

Bosco, Carmody, Elmira and I had a few drinks in the Spoon after Bosco's final evening show. I played the piano – Elmira has an old but serviceable upright near the bar – while they sat at a table just a few feet away.

Elmira had regained her color and seemed in a good mood. Too good, in fact. I was afraid she might try to sing, and that prospect generally made me a little queasy. Elmira is one of those people who are genuinely tone-deaf. People who say they are tone deaf generally are not. They have enough perception of tone to know that they are off-key. That's not the case with Elmira, who has no clue that her wounded-wildlife wails bear no resemblance to the melody.

I had to take a break to intercede in a fight, during which time Bosco took over my duties at the keyboard. He, like the piano, played serviceably. He competently but mechanically pounded out some current songs and a little light classical. That's an old trick among saloon players: When you run out of current material you can pretty much play anything as long as you give it a beat like a sad ballad or a lively two-step.

Carmody calls this "cowpoking" up the music, and for a fellow raised in a remote mountain range he somehow has picked up an encyclopedic knowledge of music and cultivated an operatic tenor that, when fueled by enough whiskey, can vibrate the windows.

I could tell what was coming when I was walking back to my spot and saw Carmody nudge Bosco with an elbow and request "something syrupy from the war."

Bosco nodded. He'd said – and although I wasn't quite sure I believed everything he told me, but I was inclined to give him the benefit of the doubt – that he'd been overseas during the war years. But the nature of being a stage performer in these parts means that you'll inevitably hear plenty of war ditties, and Bosco summoned up the first stanza of *When this Cruel War is Over*.

Bosco didn't expect Carmody to sing and was startled at the powerful tenor. His voice was almost completely devoid of accent, as often happens with singers, and possessed of a clarity that reminded me of the ringing of a bell.

> *Dearest one! do you remember,*
> *When we first did meet?*
> *When you told me how you loved me,*
> *Kneeling at my feet?*

The regulars listened respectfully, as they always do when Carmody sings. Newcomers listened in astonishment at the saintly sounds produced by the ungainly mountain man – who, even though he had lately taken to wearing suits and bowlers, still somehow wore them like overalls and a straw hat.

And I listened attentively, waiting to see how Carmody handled the political difficulties lurking in the next verse.

It's an odd song. Sentimental ballads were emotional nourishment for troops. It's hard for someone who hadn't been there to understand how closely music was woven into the lives of men on the march or fighting gnawing fear while idling in encampments or prisons. *When this Cruel War is Over* was written from a woman's point of view, but so were a lot of the songs sung by the men.

What made this one unique was its appeal to both sides, one of the few ballads I could remember that were popular in the North and the South. But of course the words were changed to fit the geography. Carmody sang it this way:

Oh! how proud you stood before me
In your suit of blue,
When you vow'd to me and country,
Ever to be true.

Well, it wasn't a surprise. Tennessee was a divided state, and Carmody's section largely sided with the Union, and Carmody himself not only was a Union scout but when he was hobbled with injuries that prevented him from shooting his weapon, he served as a color sergeant. That was the soldier – often unarmed – who carried the flag at the head of the formation and who, if wounded, was expected to pass the colors along to another before the cloth touched the ground.

If anyone took offense to Carmody's interpretation, they didn't show it, either out of the mesmerizing effect of the music or the fear of the giant with the wide shoulders and hands like as big as hams.

Carmody, who for all his combative tendencies values peaceful co-existence, at least in theory, then sang the opening stanza again but with the *Southern* version of the lyrics.

> *Oh! how proud you stood before me*
> *In your suit of grey,*
> *When you vow'd to me and country,*
> *Ne'er to go astray.*

When he finished, the was a round of applause and Bosco nodded and finished by adding a closing flourish that that was borrowed from a much earlier era and a little longer and more decorative than called for.

Carmody, not immune to stage jealousy, showed Bosco that he was not overly impressed.

"Nice touch," Camody said. It came out, *nahz tetch.* "Not sure Bach had a ballad-closer in mind when he writ that, though."

"Very good," Bosco said.

"I ain't no dummy," Carmody said.

"I can see that."

Carmody gave Bosco a tight little smile, being sure to make it clear that Bosco didn't deserve to see any teeth in this transaction, and nodded.

"It's from *Klavierbüchlein*," Carmody added.

Bosco just stared.

"It means 'piano book,'" Carmody said. "Bach writ the thing to show people how to play fancy ornaments."

I'd completed my trip back to the piano, with a detour at the bar, and Bosco seemed grateful to give up his seat at the bench and escape Carmody.

"Maybe you could show the marshal how to play a little Bach," Carmody said to Bosco. "With him spending all those years as a prizefighter he smashed them dukes of his into bags of rocks and he could use something to limber them up."

Carmody went back to the bar, searching for someone to buy him a drink in that predatory manner he adopts when thirsty, and Bosco waved me to the bench, leaned an elbow on top of the upright, and asked me what Carmody was talking about.

I told Bosco the broad strokes, how I'd started adult life as an undistinguished professor in an equally undistinguished college in Illinois, a place where I had rendered judgment on topics such as battlefield ethics even though I had never seen a battlefield. I'd had a pedestrian formal education but was a quick study, both with books and music.

But then life had changed for me and a few million other people in 1861, when I was assigned to a special unit where I'd employed trickery as well as a gun, my fists, and from time to time rocks and sticks or whatever I could find in moments of desperation.

I was a quick study in wartime, too, and this time I had to be to stay alive.

When my unit was demobilized at the end of the hostilities I returned to teaching. I can't say I missed war – no sane man would say that – but it felt like some part of me fell asleep.

But it woke up the night a strongman and pug with a traveling show called me out of a crowd and bet me long odds that I couldn't last a round with him in the ring. Normally I don't take bait like that, but he'd taunted me in front of a group of townsfolk and students.

At the same time, I felt a little rush, sort of like I imagine a bear does when he comes out of hibernation.

The pug was surprisingly quick for someone his size but I had him figured out after a minute or so, and when he dropped his left fist to dig it into my ribs, as he'd tried twice before after feinting to my head, I'd learned the steps to his dance and snaked an overhand right to his jaw that dropped him on the seat of his pants.

He was up quickly, but hurt, and ensnared me in a bear hug. That was against the rules, but given his condition I didn't mind much. When he tried to gouge out my eye, however, I took severe exception.

So I beat him to death.

I didn't have that goal in mind, exactly, but neither did I hold back out of concern for his safety. I found that while authorities in Illinois overlook prizefighting, which is technically illegal there, they are not so forgiving when somebody winds up dead. I made it out of town one step ahead of a deputy sheriff and for want of any other way to make a living, took up prizefighting. I'd done well but it's a young man's game so in a few years I moved into gun work, usually on the right side of the law. Eventually, like so many men who'd developed a new set of skills during the war but found limited opportunity to ply them in peacetime, I found myself behind a badge.

Philosophy and music, I told Bosco, were vestiges of an earlier life that belonged to a man who for all intents and purposes no longer existed.

Bosco seemed anxious to change the subject and told me that a good way to make up for loss of mobility in the hands is to practice crossing the left over the right to make up for notes a busy but impaired right hand might not be able to hit cleanly.

I felt a little flash of anger.

I was perplexed at what it was about Bosco that prodded other men into chest-thumping. Carmody is not exactly what you'd call modest, but he's not a chronic show-off either, and his rejoinder to Bosco was out of character.

I normally don't give a set of bull's balls about what other people think of me, but for whatever reason Bosco's little music lecture rubbed me the wrong way and without prelude I played *La Campanella*, by Liszt, a pianist, who wrote it to copy the violin fireworks of Paganini. It's played at a fast allegretto and several of the jumps cover two octaves.

I made no effort to cowpoke it up.

When I played, there were some wide eyes and some dropped jaws, and when I finished, there was a stunned silence.

It was so quiet, as Carmody likes to put it, you could have heard a moth piss on a pillow.

"You mean I cross over my hand like *that?*" I asked.

"Yes," Bosco said, his expression flat, and then he walked away, looking straight ahead.

The conversation around the bar and the tables picked up a little, a glass clinked here and then there, shoes scraped on the dusty wood floor, and everything returned more or less to normal, until I felt somebody pour a beer down the back of my neck.

Chapter 28

We don't have ice like the fancy bars. There's no icehouse nearby and we couldn't afford summer ice even if there was. But Elmira keeps the beer packed in sawdust, which brings it below room temperature for reasons I don't understand.

Still, the beer sliding down the back of my neck was cool enough to give me a start, and when I stopped playing and jerked around I saw the beefy kid with his hands spread in the universal gesture to indicate "I didn't mean it," and his lip curled into the half-smile that showed he really did.

"Sorry, Marshal," he said, jerking his thumb to the man next to him. "He bumped into me."

There were four of them. One was about fifty, two were somewhere in their thirties, and the one who poured the beer looked twenty, if that. He was dressed in a shirt opened halfway to his belt and his sleeves rolled up to the shoulders. An oily lock of hair hung over one eyebrow and his face had that round, meaty look of a young man whose features haven't fully formed yet.

Despite the baby fat, the face showed some flattening of the nose, some thickening of the eyelids, and enough swelling in both ears to betray his profession.

"We was leaning in close," he said, "listening to your stories about your fighting. That's why I got jostled because we was straining to hear. And that's why we come in the first place."

I knew how this scene was supposed to play out and wasn't interested in supplying any of the dialogue.

So I waited him out.

"I'm a fighter myself," he said. "Chris Bartlett. Looking for some action – bareknuckle, catch-as-catch can. Heard you been in the business and thought maybe you'd sign on for a bout. Didn't mean to start nothing. I know you got a badge and all, and you can throw me in jail or run me out of town for getting you a little wet, but I didn't come looking for no trouble."

He waited. So did I.

"Didn't mean to scare you, or scare the ladies," Bartlett said.

I saw Carmody edging toward us, and so did Bartlett.

"You don't need your friends to protect you," Bartlett said. "I was just making a sporting proposition. You can just run me out right now with that badge if I'm scaring you."

It was an interesting gambit, and didn't happen by accident. Somebody wanted to do me harm and had gone to some trouble to set things up.

Bartlett looked toward Carmody and mugged.

"You got *two* badges to flash at me," he said.

I had a feeling that the little scene was the sequel to the drama that inadvertently escalated to the Battle of Shadow Valley. It was an act of intimidation that got out of hand – which is what often happens when you threaten people with guns, especially when you threaten people who are good with guns.

Maybe whoever wanted to rough me up in the woods was trying again, this time leaving me no opportunity for gunplay.

"Am I under arrest?" Bartlett said, spreading his hands and looking around the room, which was now a silent sea of eyes.

At least I knew the strategy if not the motive. This was how they would get rid of me, or at least discredit me. They'd send a pug to call me out in front of the townspeople and beat me useless. Sure, I could shoo him and his friends, or even arrest them.

And I'd be beaten that way, too, even if nobody laid a hand on me.

"I'll bet a hundred bucks I can take you," Bartlett said, "to your twenty. Five-to-one odds. Does that get your courage up a little?"

Elmira chose that moment to bustle over start asking what was going on.

"Now you got the lady to protect you?" Bartlett said.

"No," I said, fishing a wad of bills out of my left front pocket. I didn't know exactly how much it was, and didn't care. "She's going to hold the money."

She didn't understand but took my money and stared at it.

"Give her your hundred," I said.

The beefy kid exchanged glances with the older man and I realized I'd caught them off guard, which is what I had hoped for. They were back-pedalling, now. A real manager – and I assume the fifty-year-old was the manager – would have the money ready if they really expected action.

They took a full minute to dig through their pockets and put the cash together.

They all handed it to Bartlett, who offered the wad to me.

"Want to count it?"

"Give it to the lady," I said.

"We don't hand over the stakes until we know where and when," Bartlett said.

"Here," I said. "Now."

Chapter 29

C armody knew how these affairs worked and I suppose he figured that it was best to keep things orderly.

We didn't have street lights and it was cloudy so a fight outside would be futile – and worse, not very entertaining because no one could see it – so he asked everyone to move the chairs and tables near the walls.

Protocol for a fight crowd often stipulates that everyone in the audience turn over their weapons, but trying to extract guns and knives from reluctant drunks would certainly be more dangerous than leaving things be, so Carmody let it pass. But not before making a show of hefting the shotgun he kept hidden behind the bar, just in case anybody had ideas.

I took my shirt off. Bartlett shrugged and did the same. There's generally no rule about what to wear but shirts provide an opponent with something to grab and pull, and as Bartlett had about thirty pounds on me I didn't want to give him an enhanced opportunity to wrestle with me.

While I noticed he carried some extra weight around the middle, Bartlett had thick, sloping shoulders and heavy forearms. I took him to be six-two and 230 pounds.

I could see he was sizing me up, too. He had almost two inches in height on me but my arms were longer, and if he were any good he would notice that. My stomach was flatter and my muscles were harder. I know he noticed that, but he pretended not to.

Instead, he curled his lip again.

"Are you sure you want to do this, Grandpa?"

In answer, I held up both hands, palms facing him, and rotated them to the back and then palm out again. He shrugged and showed me that his hands were empty, too.

I've been in fights where the referee recounts elaborate rules, which are, of course, immediately forgotten. Sometimes the ref would announce the maximum number of rounds, and what would cause a round to commence or end, or give instructions about when the seconds could assist their fighter, and who could call a surrender.

But because Carmody was the *de facto* referee and has little use for detail, he chose the direct approach.

"Well, *git to it*," he said.

***

Bartlett held his hands low, making little circles with his fists, and wagged his head this way and that to show me how tricky he was.

His footwork wasn't bad, but he needed some coaching on how to keep from giving away his moves. As he circled to his left and I could see him plant his rear foot as he prepared to throw his left.

So I threw a straight right over his left, really putting my legs and hips into it, and it caught him hard and by surprise.

Bartlett looked like a man who'd been hit with a piece of lumber that somebody unexpectedly thrust out a basement window.

He was out before he hit the floor. He landed flat on his back, and a cloud of that damned yellow dust swirled up into the yellow lantern-light.

Chapter 30

I'd swiped the last bottle of whiskey we had in the storeroom for myself and worked on it, brooding at my desk, while I watched the prisoners.

I wasn't in a good mood but neither was anyone else.

Bosco's final show was sparsely attended, and afterwards he stopped by the office to obliquely blame it on me because of the "climate of fear" in town that I had ostensibly failed to prevent. I was going to note that in a small, isolated town you are inevitably going to exhaust the supply of ticket-buyers, but I wanted to keep Bosco in a cooperative mood because he'd be scouting out New Paradise in the morning so I let him gripe.

Swingle was irritated with me because I put him out of his lodgings. I needed the cell for Bartlett and his three goons, who were extremely out of sorts because I'd arrested them for disorderly conduct. Now, they were well aware that I would have irrevocably lost face if I had arrested them before fighting Bartlett. But now that I'd pasted him I could do whatever I damn well felt like doing, and they knew it.

The apparently had never considered an outcome in which I survived.

Bartlett was on the cot, still making funny popping noises with his lips and twitching from time to time. I'd scrambled his brain pan pretty good. His three handlers were sitting on the floor.

The oldest one, who looked like he'd done some fighting in his day, kept squirming from time to time, looking like he had something to say.

Finally he could contain himself no more and told me that I'd landed a lucky punch because nobody could tear through Bartlett like that.

I told him that I'd be happy to let him finish the match on Bartlett's behalf.

He shut up, and pouted.

I figured I'd let them marinate in the cell for a while and maybe after a few hours of them sitting with each other's knees in their noses and Bartlett making those lip noises maybe they'd be crazy enough so I could pry loose some information about who sent them. But I wasn't hopeful. They didn't look like the chatty types. And besides, I'd stretched the boundaries of the disturbing the peace ordinance. I wasn't so sure how it would hold up in court as I was the one who eventually caused most of the disturbance.

And, of course, I had other problems to deal with, including cranky customers at the Spoon, angry because we were running out of beer and liquor.

The staff at the Full Moon were livid because I'd left them with a dead owner who looked like a macabre unicorn. I'd forgotten to take the damn pencil out of the hole in Moon's forehead.

Elmira, too, was in bad sorts because her liquor delivery had been sabotaged for a reason I had not managed to instantly and magically uncover. Also, she was not amused that I had commandeered her bar as an impromptu boxing arena.

And I was in a foul mood because I had no idea what the hell was going on.

In the past 36 hours I'd been beseeched by a frightened owner of a bar who ostensibly shot himself after writing me a letter, I'd been in the middle of a gunfight over marked cards in a saloon where I presumably kept things honest, and I'd been lured away from the same saloon by armed men while a gang sneaked in the other end of town and tried to ransack the place but were mowed down by a quick-triggered lunatic to whom I owed my life.

Just to make the day a little nicer I'd been confronted with a badly beaten man who'd had his stock of liquor – *our* stock of liquor – smashed to shards, and had come face to face with the owner of the only other bar in town who had ostensibly shot himself even though a magician couldn't have shot himself under the given circumstances, and now inexplicably challenged to a fistfight by a professional pug who just happened to be passing through town.

I still could not shake this vague queasy feeling I first experienced when I read Marner's letter and saw the report of his subsequent suicide.

I don't know what was happening, or why, in New Paradise. But I remembered, word-for-word, what Marner had written: "There are threats here from people I don't know for reasons I don't understand."

And I sure as hell didn't know what was happening, or why, here in Shadow Valley, but "threats from people I don't know for reasons I don't understand" summed it up pretty well.

Chapter 31

It was an uneventful 36 hours until Bosco returned.

I'd let Bartlett and his three goons loose the next morning. They stuck to their story that Bartlett was an itinerant prizefighter and they were his handlers and they just happened to be passing through. I'd questioned each one separately and got the same story, although the older one seemed more forthcoming. At least he told me what I took to be his real name: Bassett. It's not the kind of name you'd make up, but not so unusual it's contrived. None of them carried any identification.

Bartlett might have been the fighter's real name. It didn't matter much any more, as he'd probably answer to anything in his current condition.

The other two each, separately, told me their name was Smith.

I could have trumped up some jail-time charges against them and they knew it, but I just wanted them out of my sight and also thought that Bartlett could use some medical attention. Elmira had wrapped a bandage around his head, like a turban, though I'm not sure exactly what that was supposed to accomplish. She tried to get him to eat some soup. But he stared at the food, not quite sure what to do with it. Then he stared at the wall some more.

I felt just a little bit guilty. Granted, Bartlett had tried to do me harm but he was a fighter, and that's what fighters are paid to do, and while no fight is ever easy I could tell from the get-go he wouldn't be a real problem. There wasn't any reason to scramble his brain-pan like that.

Still, it was a hell of a punch. My hand was still a little swollen and it made a loud crackling noise whenever I flexed it, but it didn't hurt.

Another reason to let them go was to get them out of Swingle's way. Swingle kept enthusiastically offering to torture the information out of them, but I declined his offer. He seemed disappointed, but also relieved that he'd get his cell back.

So I sent them on their way at eleven.

There was a funeral for Eddie Moon at noon, and I attended with Elmira and Carmody. Carmody had been a lay preacher during the war, and while he fights occasional skirmishes with the concept of organized religion, he delivered some competent internment prayers.

It dawned on me that even though I'd been in town for a year and a half, and had personally arranged for many of the graveyard's occupants to be there, this was the first actual funeral I'd witnessed.

Moon had no family that anyone in town knew about, and as Shadow Valley was without an undertaker it had fallen upon me to do something with the body. I know nothing of embalming and am not about to learn. I'm far from squeamish, but during the war I'd been in charge of shipping soldiers' bodies home for burial and what I'd seen of the process of draining the blood and refilling the body with some sort of chemical was not appetizing.

But neither was the prospect of the body getting any riper.

So Carmody and I unfolded Moon from the chair where we'd left him and loaded him in a coffin that Carmody had assembled from lumber we were using to rebuild the rotting water-damaged wall and mirror frame in back of the bar at the Spoon.

I was going to remark on the speed with which Carmody built the coffin but stanched the impulse. Carmody's no more a sentimental man that I am a squeamish one, but he's always been reticent to expand on his grave-digging abilities and he's entitled to keep that to himself.

I couldn't help but notice, though, that he'd fashioned the coffin the way we did during the war – wider in the shoulders and narrow at the feet and head, a design that's harder to construct but uses about a quarter less wood than a rectangular casket.

Even in death, old habits die hard, I guess.

And some things are better left unsaid.

***

No one cried at Moon's funeral, not even Elmira, who is prone to weepy spells. It wasn't that
Moon was actively disliked, I suppose, but no one
particularly liked him, either. For that matter, no one
I knew even claimed to know him well.

He was just the amiably ruthless guy who
owned the bar.

He was, and now he wasn't. Simple as that.

I wondered who'd cry at my funeral but decided to think about something else.

Elmira rode back with me in the wagon and
was quiet and I wondered if she was thinking about
the same thing.

"Is there enough wood left?" she said, apro-
pos of nothing.

It took me a minute to figure out that she was
talking about the rebuilding.

"I think we'll be all right," I told her. "We
have enough to fix the rotten part near the floor and
I'm repainting the mirror instead of replacing the
frame."

"You're going to *paint* the mirror?" she said.

"Yes."

"If you paint the mirror, how will you be able
to see yourself in it?"

I took a deep breath and changed the subject.

Again, some things are better left unsaid.

Chapter 32

Bosco and Gina returned at noon the next day. I only had to look at them once to get a general idea that something very bad happened. I opened up the theater and hustled them inside.

With Swingle occupying my office and Elmira re-stocking the bar with liquor Carmody had fetched from Austin, riding shotgun while Swingle drove the wagon, there was no other convenient area that offered privacy.

While Swingle and Carmody, who were armed to the teeth and visibly in a homicidal mood, had returned unmolested, the same could not be said for Gina. Her clothes were torn in places and tied back together in an improvisational style. Her lips were swollen, and her eyes were rimmed in red and never directly met my gaze.

She wasn't crying. She was probably cried dry by now.

Bosco had that glazed look a man gets when smoldering with impotent rage. He had a black eye and I noticed that his wrists showed long, purple bruises where a rope or handcuff had cut into his flesh.

I asked just enough questions to figure out that there was no point in asking any more questions. There were three of them, and they had overtaken Bosco and Gina about halfway between New Paradise and Shadow Valley about four hours after Bosco left New Paradise to return home. From the descriptions, they could have been any of a thousand trail hands, drifters, or gamblers who bounced around these parts. In fact, the only four strangers within a hundred miles I could immediately disqualify were the ones I'd kept locked up overnight.

I asked Elmira to tend to Gina and I took Bosco for a walk to the outskirts of town. Sometimes people talk more freely when they are moving, and I had a feeling it was not going to be easy for Bosco to tell me what I needed to hear.

As it turned out, I was right in my assumption that they'd tied him up and made him watch.

I also correctly guessed that their type would have a "message" to pass along. They did. They'd told Bosco to tell me personally – and they knew my name – that I could either "get in line or get lost."

They hadn't elaborated, and Bosco had not asked. He assumed that I'd know what the remark meant, and while the specifics remained cryptic to me – I had no idea what I was supposed to do – the part about getting lost seemed clear enough.

And when they were finished with Gina, they'd told Bosco to tell me that I'd better "think about what could happen to the boss lady."

In my business you try not to take things personally. You take it for granted that you're intentionally being provoked and if you get riled you lose judgment and make yourself an easier target.

I tried to remind myself of that as I felt that little wave of lightheadedness you get when the blood pounds in your ears and that tingle of blind rage begins to crawl up the back of your neck.

Chapter 33

Bosco made me start giving him shooting lessons that afternoon.

I didn't think it was a particularly good idea. I knew how rage takes over people's minds, and putting a firearm in his hand at this moment seemed equivalent to giving a lunatic with a stick of dynamite a box of matches.

Still, I owed him. I'd sent him to Marner's bar, which accomplished nothing except to submerge him in horror. All he'd gotten at the bar was the cold shoulder or the stinkeye. All anybody would say was that the place was under "new management."

Then two goons had roughed him up and tossed him out between the batwings.

And on the way back, as a result of my assignment, he'd faced, unarmed, a situation where resisting could only have gotten him killed.

For some men, living with a memory like that is worse than death. I suppose it depends on how they follow up.

So I fitted Bosco out with a Colt I'd lifted off one of the men Swingle had massacred. My office tends to become over-run with confiscated firearms, so I told Bosco he could keep it.

Bosco knew nothing about guns. He told me he had nothing against firearms, per se. It was simply that growing on in an Eastern city they'd not been part of his life, nor had they been readily available in Europe.

I started his practice with an unloaded weapon, holstered in a rig I'd also taken off a dead man. His unfamiliarity with weapons was obvious, and under other conditions I might have ribbed him about it, but it was not a time for humor.

So we both set about our task with grim determination.

Every man has a different idea about where a gun is easy to reach. Despite what you read in the dime novels, there's not a lot of fancy holstering or trickery associated with a draw, at least among people who play the game for real. Some of the fastest and deadliest men I've known kept the damn things in their front pockets. I've known other accomplished shootists who've kept pistols in their waistbands, or sashes, or drew from across their body, or kept the weapons tucked in the small of their back.

Bosco asked me where the best place to carry a gun was, and I told him that was like asking a chess player what "the best move in the world" is. It all depends on the situation.

The way I did it, I told him, was as good as any and better than most, so we might as well start there.

His weapon had a 7-and-a-half-inch barrel, fairly long, but he was tall and had big hands and the longer barrel adds to accuracy. Being able to hit what you aim at is more important than getting the shot off fast.

The holster I'd appropriated for him had been modified at some time, with a little of the leather on the back trimmed down to slide the gun out faster. In theory, that's a good idea but it also leads to the gun dropping out of the holster when you lean back in a chair. Everything involves a trade-off.

Bosco seemed most comfortable with thumbing the hammer back as he drew, rather than fanning with his left, a good approach in my book because fanning is hard on the action and a jammed gun is worse than no gun at all because it will induce people to shoot at you when you have no way of firing back.

I immediately broke him of a bad habit: He tended to pull the gun out of the holster with his finger on the trigger, which is a foolproof technique for shooting yourself in the leg.

He was an astonishingly quick study. His magician's dexterity gave him an obvious advantage, and, perhaps most importantly, he knew how to practice. He practiced like I practice an unfamiliar piece on the piano, starting slowly, getting the action down individual movement by individual movement, and then putting it all together and picking up the speed.

Bosco adapted well to leaning way back when he shot. Not everyone can pull this off but he was quick and limber. If you lean back and bring the shoulders high when you draw you speed up the process of getting the gun out of the holster and level to the ground. I also told him that once the gun cleared the holster, he should concentrate on the feeling of dropping his shoulder *down* rather than lifting the forearm *up*. It's a more powerful and natural movement and brings the weapon into shooting position faster.

I tried to train him to turn sideways as he drew, but it wasn't his type of motion. Bodies are different and his just didn't twist that way. For me, presenting a smaller target is well worth the extra split-second it takes to turn. In fact, I told him, getting a good aim is worth additional time, too. I've seen one gunman, who was actually rather slow on the draw, assume the side-stance dueling position and take careful aim while all six of his opponent's shots – fired with blinding speed but fired basically blind – went wild. The slowpoke finished it with one well-placed bullet to the chest.

We kept at it for about two hours. I was getting hungry and my hand was getting blistered and I told Bosco that he should knock off. You can't learn this stuff in a day – through truth be told he had picked up in an afternoon what some men never absorb in a lifetime. Bosco knew how to manipulate things with his hands, and he possessed cat-quick agility and reflexes.

Bosco said I could leave, but he was going to stay in the field we'd chosen for the lesson and practice until dark.

But first he wanted to draw against me. To see how good he was.

I told him again that it wasn't really the speed of the draw that counted and the important part would come when he practiced hitting a target with live bullets.

Undeterred, he asked if we couldn't try it with blanks or something and I demurred and told him that blanks were dangerous too and could do a very efficient job of blinding you if the shot went to the face.

Bosco insisted.

We'd just make sure the guns were empty and dry-fire, he implored. I was getting tired of this posturing, I countered, and dry-firing is tough on the mechanism.

Bosco was not to be denied. I respected his intentions, and admired his facility with his hands, but was getting me a little peeved by his belief that gunfighting was like a stage trick he could master in an afternoon.

So I unloaded my weapon, double-checked it, and double-checked his, too, even though I knew it was empty. I'm superstitious.

And then we stood an arm's length apart and I told him to draw first and I'd react.

He was smooth. His face did not betray his intentions. Some people squint or flinch when they are about ready to pull but he kept his features placid as a statue.

He didn't dig for the gun. His downward motion was smooth and he formed his grip instantly and he leaned back just like I'd shown him and he damn near had the holster cleared when the tip of my barrel made contact with the center of his forehead.

I pushed a little harder than I had to, and he leaned back.

Then I pulled the trigger, and the hammer clicked home.

He flinched, nodded, and went back to practicing as I walked back to town.

Chapter 34

It was turning into a wonderful damned day. When I turned the corner, I saw that a crowd had formed in the street outside the Spoon.

The same three I'd let out of jail eight hours ago were back, minus Bartlett, who was probably still staring at a wall somewhere, playing with his lips.

In Bartlett's stead was a bald man, stripped to the waist, who had a bullet-shaped head and a chest with thick, rounded muscles extending like cannon-balls over the bulge of his belly.

Bassett stepped forward.

"We come to set things straight," he said.

I was going to ask him what the hell he was talking about but figured there was no need to encourage him, and I was right. He lifted his hat and brushed back a lock of lank sandy hair that had fallen over his eyes, which were bloodshot and baggy.

He set the hat back squarely on his square head and drilled he with those hound-dog eyes and loudly accused me of being a ringer and a hustler and luring Bartlett into a fight he wasn't ready for.

And now the poor kid was sitting in his room playing with his lips.

Bassett was a pretty good liar. Experienced liars learn that generally the more absurd and outrageous the lie, the more likely people are to believe it. And the more you wail about the injustice of it all, even if you're lying out your ass, the more people will believe. The more they'll *want* to believe it.

I figured I should at least offer some token resistance.

"For the record," I said, "you showed up out of nowhere and your man picked the fight with me and he said he did it because he'd heard me bragging, which for the record didn't happen either."

"Keep saying that long enough," Bassett said, "and maybe you'll believe it yourself. But nobody here will."

I heard boots scraping on the powdery street, which was packed hard as stone from a month without rain. I looked around to find that the crowd had swelled to maybe fifty people, most of whom I didn't know. The ratio is pretty typical for a town where drifters make up the half of the population that replaces itself every week or so.

"What do you want?" I said.

"Only what's fair," Bassett said. "Even money, two hundred dollars, with a real fighter, not some kid you hustled."

"And who is this?" I asked, pointing at the bullet-head.

"My name's John Ivey," the bullet-head said, smiling with his mouth and hating with his eyes. "From Wichita. You heard of me?"

"No," I said. "Who put you up to this?"

The question caught him by surprise. Ivey hesitated and shot a quick look at Bassett before he remembered that grown-up fighters don't let other men speak for them and told me it was none of my business.

I turned to Bassett.

"You've gone to a lot of trouble to rough me up in front of the townsfolk," I said, "and find a way to do it that looks legal. It didn't work out for you before and it won't this time, either."

"Kiss my ass, Grandpa," Ivey said.

I ignored him. I pegged him to be ten years younger than I, but wasn't really sure. With those craggy stone-faces you can't always tell.

"Bassett," I said, "what's behind all this?"

"Let's just say that there are people who think it's time for you to move on. Times change, and you can change with them or get out of the way."

"I have no idea what you're talking about," I said, and it was true.

"Hey," Ivey said, "all that concerns us right now is whether you're man enough pony up the two hundred." The smile was just as wide but the eyes were narrower.

"Or you can chicken out," Bassett said. "Stick with beating up kids. Your choice. I'd like to tell you that no one would think less of you, but they would."

Bassett magnetized everybody's attention with his flow of bullshit so effectively that none of us noticed that Carmody had elbowed his way through the crowd. He walked past Bassett, stuck out his arm, and shoved Ivey so hard that the big man fell on the seat of his pants.

Chapter 35

Ivey stayed down, reached behind him, lifted himself on his palms, and raised one foot, poised to kick. That worried me. It showed that he really knew what he was doing. You expose yourself when you try to regain your feet. On your hands with a foot in the air you're in a strong defensive position if you're only dealing with one attacker.

Carmody stayed out of range of Ivey's boot and pointed to his badge.

"I'm a deputy marshal," he said, "and I'm not involved in whatever game you two is playing. I got no stake in this other than keeping the peace. And if you don't think I can come up with some way to arrest you, let me tell you I have a damned vivid imagination. I'll put you in a cell right now."

"But I just moved my stuff back in," piped Swingle's testy tenor.

A couple bystanders were genuinely intrigued by Swingle's lament but refocused their attention on the main show.

Carmody wanted to up the tension. He kicked a plume of dirt in Ivey's direction, put his hand on the butt of his revolver, and took a step closer. Ivey forgot about his pasted-on menacing smile and emitted a jungle-cat snarl.

I caught Carmody's eye for a second and nodded in a way only he would notice and he did the same. After more than a year dodging bullets together, Carmody and I have a mind-reading act better than Bosco's.

Carmody had accomplished two things. First, he'd given me a chance to back out with some grace. If, in his legitimate capacity as a law enforcement officer, he was determined to break up a public spectacle and start arresting people, I had a plausible excuse to go along with the act.

Second, if I intended to bite at Bassett's bait, Carmody had unsettled Ivey, gotten him rattled, made him angry, and taken him off his game.

"So this is how it's going to play out?" Bassett said. "Your deputy riding to your rescue? You're backing off?"

"Backing off what?" I said.

"Two hundred dollars, even money," Bassett said. "You in or out?"

"Out," I said.

Bassett turned his head and raised it a little so he could give me the slant-eye.

"I thought more of you, Hawke," he said.

"How much more?" I said.

He didn't know what to make of that.

"How much more?" I repeated.

Bassett just looked at me, his mask of contrived contempt melting into an expression of confusion.

"How about three hundred dollars more?" I said. "Up the bet. I'll fight your man for five hundred dollars. Take it or leave it."

Chapter 36

They only had $380 dollars between them so I agreed that I would put my five hundred against their cash, both their horses, and their guns. I hadn't seen their horses and didn't need another horse, and I have so many confiscated guns that I could start my own gun shop, but the bet gave me a mental edge. I could afford to lose the five hundred, but Bassett and Ivey would surely feel a gnawing worry in the back of their minds about how they were going to get back to Austin, or Wichita, or wherever they were really from, on foot, with no money and no sidearms.

But after all the bravado they spouted, there was no way that they could turn me down.

Carmody, who was a born hustler and promoter, could not have been more joyful. He scheduled the bout to start in a half-hour outside the bank, where the road was wide and was bordered by a hill where spectators could stand for an unobstructed view.

During the rainy season the bank area, which is on a delta of two streams, is prone to severe flooding, a fact which always made me wonder about the judgment of the bankers who built or rebuilt it there several times. Most recently, they moved the building back to its original foundations after a torrent of water had nudged it loose and carried it across the street. Before that, they rebuilt it from the ground up after a flood, and prior to that they fixed it up after I had accidentally burned it down. But that's not the fault of bad engineering and is a story for another time.

But now, in mid-October, the bowl-shaped area was hard and flat and dusty, even though you could still detect a dank and musty odor from the fetid delta a hundred feet away.

Carmody had taken it upon himself to set up the ring, which he improvised by nudging back the front row of spectators until he'd created a human circle about 25 feet in diameter.

He'd also sent a kid to fetch two stools from the Spoon, and the boy returned with the chairs and their owner. Elmira, I noted, was wearing that icy look she affects to show me that something I've done displeased her.

But I know it's really the expression she pastes on to hide it when she's scared.

And as I sat on my stool, taking a good look at the ape named Ivey, I didn't blame her one bit.

Chapter 37

Bassett held the money and Carmody refereed.

Carmody toed a scratch line in the dirt between me and Ivy, and recited his version of the London Prize Ring rules, the version commonly recited and then largely ignored in bareknuckle matches around here: No biting, hitting a man when he's down, or striking with foreign objects held in the hands. Kicking is allowed unless the opponent is down. The round ends when a fighter hits the ground because of a blow or a throw, and resumes after a thirty-second rest period. After each round Carmody will make a new scratch line and if a fighter could not be up to scratch the opponent would win. There were no seconds to assist fighters between rounds, and only a fighter himself could surrender.

Carmody then turned to the crowd, which had materialized from nowhere. Fights draw drifters like a sugar cube draws ants. There must have been more than a hundred people sitting and standing, the ones facing west painfully squinting into the glare of the slanting late-afternoon October sun. A few had brought liquor with them, and an enterprising young man was selling bags of peanuts.

"Your wagers is your own business," Carmody announced. "I will referee the bout but will not settle disputes over bets. All I'll say on the subject is that all bets are off if the bout is called on account of darkness, which is probably two hours from now so I ain't too worried about that. All bets are off if the bout is stopped because of a raid by law enforcement, and since the only law enforcement here is me and one of the fighters, I don't see that happening, neither."

Carmody had either refereed before or had seen a lot of fights, or maybe he'd been in a few prize matches. He'd never mentioned any involvement with fighting, even though we'd talked about it a lot and he knew that I'd spent almost a decade fighting in rings, warehouses, and wide spots in the road across from Ohio to Arizona.

He's by no means the silent type but he likes to keep secrets.

I made a note to find out more about his past later, if I still had my senses.

Chapter 38

It had been five or six years since I'd been in a prize fight, unless you count the one punch I threw against Bartlett.

Don't get me wrong, in my job I get in fights pretty much every week and some are pretty serious, but it's not the same thing as a prolonged match against a trained opponent.

I had no idea if Ivey was any good but it stood to reason that whoever would go to all this trouble to see that I got the tar stomped out of me would invest in some talent, especially after I'd flattened the first thug sent to do the job.

Ivey looked like he could do the job, though. His eyes and big jug ears bore the appropriate scars, which are not necessarily the sign of a tough guy. Scars are actually the stigmata of somebody who gets hit a lot. Nevertheless, they indicate a healthy level of experience.

And when the action started, I saw that he moved well. Ivey circled to my left and crouched, forcing me to guard against the possibility he might rush me and grab a leg or pick me up around the waist and slam me down.

I didn't want to wrestle with him so I started popping him with long left jabs.

I landed three hard ones, but he lowered his head each time and all I hurt was my hand.

The son of a bitch had a skull thick as a bank vault and he just crouched and absorbed them on that gleaming bullet of a head.

Ivey rushed me and I drew my right leg back and leaned forward, which is what he wanted me to do. He wasn't trying to grab me, but he wanted me to think that he was. Instead, he intended to bury that thick head in my chest and then bring it up under my chin.

It almost worked but I was able to plant a panicky elbow on the back of his neck, preventing him from uppercutting me with his misshapen cranium, and then I brought a knee up and caught him in the face.

He backed off and so did I.

Ivey absently drew the back of his left hand across his nose, noted the smear of blood, and smiled.

"Nice move," he said, and then suddenly hit me with a looping right.

I managed to tuck in my chin and take most of it with my shoulder but that's something you don't want to do very often because a hard blow to the socket can numb your arm. A guy who punches as hard as Ivey might even break the bone.

Ivey had my attention focused on that big right hand and he knew it so he tried to kick me in the knee. He was slow about it, though, and I checked the kick by turning my foot sideways, which meant that the force of his kick would drive his shin into the side of my heel.

He did a good job hiding it but I could tell he was hurt. He was wearing low boots that didn't cover much of his ankle or shin and he'd connected solidly with the rigid edge of my boot-heel.

Ivey danced backward, taking some weight off the injured limb and buying some time to shake off the pain in his shin.

Some people are just sensitive down there, but I had a feeling that Ivey wasn't much of a kicker and had never trained for it. Shins are funny: You take enough hits there, or deliver enough, and they eventually toughen up like axe handles.

Ivey was also built like an egg on toothpicks. He wasn't what you'd call fat, but he had a big waist and hips and kicking probably didn't come naturally to him because it wouldn't be easy for him to get a leg very high in the air. He was a straight-in, kick-to-the-knee and butt-with-the-head specimen.

I snapped out another side-kick and caught him in the same spot on the shin and he almost buckled.

I tried it again and I knew he would be very interested in not absorbing a third blow and I was right; he was ready for it and he obediently snagged my foot with both hands.

And that's when I knew I had him.

Chapter 39

I used to know a sailor named Loomis who'd traveled through Siam and done some fighting there. They are clever fighters, the Siamese, and they'd taught Loomis what they call "the art of the eight limbs."

The Siamese are sort of verbally imaginative because knees, elbows, feet, and hands aren't really limbs, but that's beside the point.

The point is that they can kick like mules. One of the tricks Loomis taught to me was a snapping roundhouse kick where you spin your whole body and dig your shin into the thigh of your opponent. He called it a "trick" when he taught it to me and I did, too, after I'd learned it, but there's no real trick to it. You just practice the kick until you can whip it with tremendous power and your shin toughens up to the point where you can break somebody's thigh with it.

Loomis told me that in Siam the first lesson he'd learned – the hard way – was that you defend against legs with legs. If somebody tries to shin-kick you, you block it with your shin, and may the best shin win.

You never try to block a kick with your hands or arms because you'll wind up with a broken hand or arm, and if you do manage to catch the kick without absorbing damage, you'll tie up your hands in the process.

Ivey didn't know that. He scooped up my foot and tried to hold it aloft, like a trophy, expecting me to topple backward.

It never occurred to him that I could easily hop around on one foot while he lifted his arms and exposed his lower ribs, which I gratefully broke with a nasty right hook.

I could actually hear one or more of those floating ribs snap. While some men have thicker skulls than others, I think all ribs are created equal and his were shattered. He dropped his elbow to shield his side from another blow, letting loose of my foot.

I brought the right high this time and caught him on the point of his chin. It was a glancing blow, and he was able to absorb some of it by rolling along with it, but he'd raised his left hand – too late – to defend his face and left those ribs unprotected again and I beat him like a drum, digging deeply into the same spot.

Ivey grunted and sunk to his knees.

Chapter 40

Carmody shouted out the time.

"Thirty seconds," he said. It came out, *thartee sekkins.*

Ivey wasn't smiling any more. He was hurt and probably couldn't move his left arm but he still had that powerful right hand and that sledgehammer of a head.

A lot of times a downed fighter will jump back to his feet to show that he wasn't really hurt, whether he was or not, but Ivey was going to take every second and try to get his breath back.

Carmody made a show of scrutinizing his pocket watch to show that everything was on the up-and-up.

"Twenty seconds."

Elmira had bought him that watch to replace one that had been broken when he'd intervened in a fight at the Spoon, and I'd helped her pick it out and knew for a fact that it had no second hand, but I felt no need to make an issue out of it.

"Ten seconds," Carmody said, after what seemed like ten minutes.

Ivey was getting his breathing back to normal and had a clear focus in his eyes and I wondered if Carmody was dragging this out for dramatic effect.

Or maybe he'd secretly bet on Ivey.

Ivey planted his right hand deep in the dirt and heaved himself up, keeping his left elbow pinned against his ribs.

Then Carmody used his heel to dig out a scratch line and Ivey and I faced off.

And as soon as Carmody told us to resume Ivey took a handful of dirt he'd balled up in his fist and threw it in my eyes.

Chapter 41

If a roomful of chemists had sat down and tried to invent a potion to blind me, they probably could not have improved on the sharp and dusty granules on Front Street. It felt like a swarm of microscopic bees were stinging my eyeballs, and even when I forced my eyes open all I could see were cloudy smudges.

I wondered if Carmody was going to intercede but he didn't, and I suppose there was no point. Rules really didn't count much in this environment, and in any event his admonition at the beginning of the bout covered *striking* with a foreign object in the hand, like weights or brass knuckles. There was nothing about throwing dirt.

I could have taken a knee and received the 30-second break, but Ivey forestalled that strategy by grabbing me around the waist before I had time to react and was battering me with his head, swiping like a metronome, rocking me with rhythmic blows to the sides of my jaw.

He wasn't going to let me fall down before he'd put my lights out, and as he was practically lifting me off the ground I couldn't get a footing to execute a throw or push him off me.

And just to add to my frustration, Carmody started talking – more loudly than seemed necessary or, for that matter, humanly possible – to somebody in the crowd about how it's smart to fight with the head. Carmody recited a loud and gleeful story about how he had once bested me with the same tactic.

Two things were wrong about what he said. Yes, Carmody and I had been in a fight once, a real barn-burner, where I was trying to physically restrain him from accepting a challenge to a gunfight I knew he couldn't win. But he wasn't fighting like Ivey. He was butting me low, trying to lift me off the ground, not battering from side to side. And also, he didn't get the best of it. I broke his grip by...

And then it occurred to me that Carmody talks a lot but rarely without a reason.

I had broken his grip by smacking my palms over his ears.

I'd hated to do that to Carmody because you can do some serious and permanent damage, and as I was trying to keep him from getting killed it didn't make sense to kill him in the process – but at the time Carmody was preparing to ram me through a wall and it was the last item in my bag of tricks.

I was still blind from the dirt in my eyes, but even though I couldn't see, I had no trouble finding Ivey's head because he was still trying to forcibly insert it into mine.

I could hear the popping when I clapped my palms perfectly over the ears, as hard I as could manage, with enough force to pop his eardrums.

Ivey screamed and tried to pull down and away, but I held onto him. If he moved back and was able to attack me again I'd still be blind and defenseless.

But right now, in a clinch, his eyesight didn't give him an advantage.

We were even.

I gripped his left ear with all my strength, to the point where he'd have had to rip it off if he wanted to pull away. I snaked my right hand over the back of his neck and forced his head downward and came up with my knee.

Siamese fighters make a specialty of that move. Usually they interlace their fingers on the back of the neck and generate tremendous impact yanking the head down while striking up with the knee.

***

Fight spectators are generally a loud and bloodthirsty lot when they get caught up in the event. It was lucky for a few of them that I was temporarily blinded because I heard more than a few of them cheering Ivey on as he pulverized my head. If they were regulars in town, and I had seen their faces, I'm not sure I would have forgiven them too easily or too quickly.

But now there was no noise.

When I connected with the knee, and as I followed up three, four times, with half my rage and pain channeled into raising my knee and the other half flowing into the effort to jerk Ivey's head down into the path of the knee, it was strangely silent.

I only heard a few gasps after my knee crunched home.

After the third knee connected, I heard a woman's voice, presumably Elmira's, say, "Oh, my god."

And the last thing I heard before I passed out was Carmody's voice.

"Goddamn it," he said, "you're sticking that knee into *me*. It's over."

Chapter 42

I've always hated boats, especially when they're sinking.

Only twice was I onboard a floating vessel in the war, and both times they were shot to pieces. The second time, it was a troop transport that sunk and damn near dragged me to the bottom with it.

I could feel the sting of the water as it forced its way up my nose, and the rising panic as I tried to push aside wooden fragments of the boat that floated between me and the surface. They were astonishingly heavy and seemed to have a will of their own, floating back between me and the surface in a malicious, conspiratorial way.

I never quite mastered the trick of keeping my eyes open underwater. The water stung but even though I was drowning everything seemed punishingly bright and the water exerted a painful pressure, like thumbs thrusting into my eyes.

I was gasping for air and sensed that this would be my last shot to make the surface and I raked my arm in front of me, trying to clear away the floating debris.

I hit something and somehow it gripped my arm.

Then Carmody told me that if I hit the other fighters as much as I hit the referee I'd be, as he put it, the *world champeen.*

He poured one more bucket of water into my face as I came to.

Everything was a little blurry but surprisingly my eyes didn't sting much. Or maybe they did but my head hurt so badly that I didn't notice.

I clearly remembered everything up to the last knee I'd delivered to Ivey's face, but everything was a little murky after that. Carmody told me that I'd put Ivey out cold with the first shot but kept hold of his head and pummeled him until Bassett intervened, and then I'd kneed Bassett, as Carmody put it, right in the old engine room, and then I'd blindly charged around looking for people to knee and tagged a few, including Carmody, before those accumulated shots to the temple added up and I took a brief dirt nap.

I sat up, keeping the palms of both hands on the ground in back of me. I felt a little queasy but I had my bearings.

Most of the crowd was still there, and they started to cheer and applaud.

I waved but when I lifted the hand that was bracing me I flopped back.

Things got cloudy for a second or two and then Elmira's face was directly overhead. It was hard to read her expression because it was upside down. But I gathered she was concerned.

"Did he hit you hard?" she said, holding her hand to her mouth.

It wasn't a complicated answer but it was such a bizarre question that I couldn't, at the moment, come up with a strategy to answer it appropriately, so I let my eyes swim around until I found Carmody again.

"But I won, and they paid up, right?"

"Sure, you was awake and charging about for a good two minutes after you put Ivey out. I tried to raise your hand but got a knee in the neighborhood of my private parts for my trouble."

"Sorry," I said. "Bassett paid?"

"Once he could walk," Carmody said, "Bassett handed over the money. Now he's trying to wake up his fighter but all the bald guy does is stare right at the sun. I think you rearranged his marbles permanent."

I tried sitting up again and this time it was easier.

The applause started up again and I waved again and didn't fall back in the dirt.

"Can I hold the money?" I asked Carmody.

He raised an eyebrow but nodded and pulled out a wad of cash the size of a head of lettuce. I took it, stood up in shaky, newborn-colt way, and held the wad over my head.

Carmody spoke in a low voice.

"I never knowed you to care one snip about money," he said. "You made a lot more than this from bounties and rewards, and you just kept the envelopes sitting in your drawer until Elmira got nervous and took it to the bank for you."

"That was different," I said.

"How?" Carmody said.

"That was money I earned."

"And?"

"This is money I *won*. There's a difference."

He smiled and told me he got it. It came out, *ahh git it.*

And then he winked and I winked back and I took a deep breath and it hurt to breathe. I was stabbed by white-hot pain. Everywhere.

I could barely keep my balance.

And I felt better than I'd ever felt in my life.

Chapter 43

After a bath and a couple beers I felt even better.

It had been a productive day. I'd won $380, two plug-ugly horses and two guns so decrepit I would be afraid to shoot them for fear of them exploding on me.

But I'd wailed the snot out of a good fighter and in the process wrung the truth out of Bassett.

Faced with the possibility of walking to Austin – which might, I supposed, take a month – accompanied by a jug-eared pug who could not yet form sentences, with no money and no gun to defend himself or put an end to his misery, should it come to that, Bassett became more talky that a dozen barbers.

Especially after I took him to the Spoon and fed him half a dozen whiskeys and assured him that this was business and there were no hard feelings.

I learned that Bassett actually was a fight promoter. He knew too much detail to be making it all up. He had a stable of pugs and aspiring tough guys in Austin and sometimes hired them out between fights as muscle – bouncers, strike-breakers, loan collectors, and the like.

A tall man with a pointy face who called himself Ludd had started hiring Bassett's fighters about six months ago. Word had it, Bassett said, that Ludd was also recruiting gunmen for more serious and apparently more permanent solutions to whatever his problem might be. Word further had it, Bassett explained, that Ludd set up a chain of command and recruited some experienced career criminals to become *de facto* captains of the gangs.

Bassett said he didn't know what the whole business was about, that Ludd never told him, and that maybe Ludd didn't really know the whole story himself. I believed Bassett. Anybody with the resources and wherewithal to start an organized criminal enterprise would certainly be smart enough to keep things compartmentalized.

Bassett speculated that Ludd was a mid-level operator because he occasionally referred to demands imposed by "The Man."

That's all they ever call him. The Man.

I asked if this were the same "Man" who set up the aborted rampage in the Spoon, and Bassett said he had no idea but it was plausible because Bassett's muscle had been deployed to bust up a number of bars.

Including one in a place called New Paradise?

Including one in a place called New Paradise, Bassett said.

I poured Bassett another shot and took one myself. I'm leery of drinking too much after getting hit in the head – conventional wisdom among fighters says it's dangerous, but no one can exactly say why – but I was getting that glow that drowned out my internal voice of caution.

Besides, I hurt all over and short of a dose of laudanum, which I avoided because of what I'd seen it to do people who weren't careful with their dosages or their habits, I didn't know of a better way to kill the pain of a beating than old-fashioned whiskey. The stuff that we'd bought to replace the smashed-up order was actually palatable. In fact, there was an outside chance it was distilled from some actual rye. Elmira's bargain brand was, I suspected, largely concocted from molasses, grain alcohol, and tobacco juice.

Bassett gazed into the amber liquid for a full minute while he apparently pondered whether he was going to tell me what was on his mind.

When people spend time chewing their cuds over whether they should tell you something, I believe they usually will, if you let them. You keep your mouth shut during the time they take to convince themselves. If you interrupt you'll nudge them off their own rails.

"You don't seem like a bad guy, Marshal," he said, "Maybe it's because I handle fighters, and you was a fighter, and even though none of us is saints we follow sort of a code."

I nodded and kept my mouth shut and let him tell the story his own way.

"There's something big going on," he said after what may have been five minutes. "I only see one little sliver of light from a lantern in the dark and I don't know what the rest of the picture is. I don't know who the players are but they ain't good people. I ain't exactly good people myself so I got keen instincts."

I nodded.

"Like you say, none of us are saints."

"Anyway," Bassett said, "all I know for sure is that whoever they is, they don't like you. One time Ludd had somebody with him and they was talking on the boardwalk, real quiet-like, right outside the cigar store I go to sometimes. They didn't know I was inside the store. The window was open and I happened to be right next to it. Your name came up."

He had my attention.

"You told me that a bunch rode into town to ransack your girlfriend's bar. I didn't have nothing to do with that. But Ludd did. He must have known about it because he told the fellow he was with that The Man didn't want no more gunplay with you or any of the other maniacs in the town. No offense. Them are his words, not mine."

"No offense taken," I said.

"So that's why he was coming to me for a fighter, to put you in your place and maybe bust you up so bad you wouldn't make trouble. But no guns. The Man didn't want you dying by a bullet because that attracts attention. And you and the rest of the…"

"Maniacs," I offered.

"Yeah, you and the rest of the maniacs is too good with guns to bother with."

I nodded and kept my gaze on the bar.

"When Ludd came to me later that day I gave him that kid Bartlett. He's strong and mean and actually likes putting a beating on people. Ludd told me that he'd checked on you and you was good with a gun but too old to fight much anymore."

I started to say something but changed my mind.

"Well, when Ludd found out you got in that one punch against Bartlett he was madder than a stuffed toad and told me to get somebody who could do the job or he'd burn my place down. So I made a deal with another promoter. I actually lost money on the arrangement, not even counting what I lost on the bet, and bought Ivey. He ain't never been beat but once."

"Twice," I said, abandoning my strategic silence.

"Yeah, twice."

I turned and faced him head-on.

"Bassett, I need to ask you a question. I have to know this, and if you are responsible and admit to it I'll let it pass. And if you lead me in the right direction I'll never mention that I got the information from you."

Bassett thought about it and said that would be all right.

It pained me to make a devil's deal. But part of this case cried out for justice, and I couldn't think of any other way to get the lead I needed.

"I sent a man named Bosco to New Paradise to find out what happened at a bar owned by a guy named Gus Marner. Do you know anything about that?"

"Couple of my boys went there to stir up a bar fight, yes."

I tensed up. I didn't care about the bar fight. I could let that pass.

"Marner was found shot, suicide, they say, but I'm not sure it went down that way."

"Didn't have nothing to do with anything more than a few busted noses and chairs, I swear," Bassett said. "Don't know nothing about no suicide."

I believed him. I'm not exactly sure why, but he seemed to have faith that I would keep my word and I was offering him absolution and that seemed to mean something to him. All I could do was allow myself to be steered by my gut.

"There's been other trouble," I said. "A load of liquor we bought was smashed up. Did you have anything to do with that?"

"Yep," he said. "Ludd told me where and when and I sent some tough guys to do the job. Just break stuff and rough up the driver. Ludd didn't tell me why and I didn't ask, but you know as well as I do that nobody goes to the trouble of busting up inventory unless they've got something they want to sell instead."

Bassett shook his head and told me he was sorry.

"I'm not mad about that, nor particularly concerned," I said, although that wasn't entirely true. "You're off the hook. But I've got one more question to ask, and it's the same deal. Tell the truth, and that's the end of it."

I didn't sell too hard. He'd admitted to the wagon attack, so he'd gotten in the habit of telling me the truth.

So I took a deep breath and asked the question casually, like it didn't really matter.

"When this Bosco was coming back from New Paradise, he had a girl with him. Some men roughed him up and took advantage of the girl. Do you know anything about that?"

Bassett straightened up and gave me a hard look.

***

It's interesting how people get their view of the world backward. I'm from Illinois, and I've spent time in Chicago and big cities in the East. Lots of people in the cities don't know any better and think that all folks in the West are basically savages, which in some ways is true, but it's the case that a woman is more likely to get groped in the street or otherwise disrespected in Chicago than anywhere around here.

Bump into a woman on the street in Shadow Valley and you tip your hat and say you're sorry or else even the drifters will take it upon themselves to teach you some manners.

Bassett looked like he had taken offense and wanted to say something sharp to me but his expression softened and he spoke in a low tone.

"No, I did not. I can tell you that I'm not the kind of person who would have anything to do with that sort of thing. But I'm working for Ludd and I can't say the same for him. So I got no right to get on a high horse."

"But you don't know anything about it?"

"No."

"Can you find out?"

Bassett thought for a second.

"I got to tread careful around Ludd. When he threatened to burn my place down he *meant* it. And it came so casual that I think he's got the means to do it – him and The Man he talks about."

"I understand that," I said, "but if you hear things you can pass them along to me. Nothing will get back to Ludd, or to this 'Man,' from me."

"Can't promise nothing," Bassett said. "For one thing, when I get back and tell him you beat Ivey into pudding he might burn my place down anyway. I don't know what's next for me. Or for you. But I'll keep my ear to the ground."

"I'll appreciate that. Just listen."

"No," Bassett said, giving himself a hard look in the still-unpainted mirror, "I'll make it my damn business to find out."

"Thanks."

"Now I want to ask you a question, if you don't mind."

I said he could.

"That dirt Ivey threw in your eyes," he said, "wasn't my idea. But the guy was desperate. You probably busted his ribs."

"I know I did," I said. "I heard them crack."

"Up until the time he threw that dirt in your lamps, you was handling him pretty easy. That was my impression, anyway. If the fight would have gone on without Ivey riling you up, would you have put him away without too much trouble?"

"You know as well as I do that it's impossible to say. One punch, one kick, an inch either way, can change the whole business in a flash. And Ivey's got hands like stones."

Bassett nodded.

"I am aware of that," he said. "But what's your general feeling, just between us? Would you have finished him easy?"

"Probably," I said.

"How old are you?"

It caught me by surprise. Everybody seemed obsessed with my age all of a sudden.

"I'll be 45 in a couple weeks."

"Ain't that old," Bassett said, easing his way back into my good graces. "The best fighter in these parts, John Stokes, is only two years younger than you."

Bassett shook his head.

"Imagine that," he said. "Almost as old as *you*."

He was beginning to veer out of my zone of good graces so I asked him what his question was.

"There's lots of titles and such, but Stokes calls himself Champion of the West, and he makes big purses. And he's close to your age."

"Again, your question is?"

Bassett paused for a second, looking me up and down.

"You got any more fight left in you?" he said.

"I do all right in lawing," I said. "I get my hat shot off every once in a while, but on the whole it's an easier way to make a living that eating knuckles."

Bassett finished his drink, fished a card out of his breast pocket, wiped the forever-wet bar with his elbow, and carefully placed the card in the dry spot.

"If you change your mind," he said, "here's where to reach me."

Chapter 44

I woke up the next day with a headache, blurry eyes, and a sense of urgency.

During the night, I dreamed about lanterns in the darkness, and I realized that I'd been fixating on Bassett's remark about seeing things in slivers of lantern-light but not getting the whole view.

We'd used special lanterns during the war. They had sliding shields and you actually could focus a small arc of light so you could see in front of you but people to the side and back couldn't see you, or at least not very well. I dreamed about them.

I also dreamed about seeing elephants in the lantern light – maybe because it felt like an elephant had stepped on my head, or maybe because my battered brain had recalled a fable I'd heard once about blind men who had never seen an elephant before and encountered one in the dark. By feel, one concluded that the elephant was like a rope because the blind man was grasping its tail. Another guessed it was a tree because he felt the elephant's leg.

I was in the middle of a puzzle with a lot of elephant parts revolving around me and I sensed that something evil and ominous was about to unload on me but I couldn't put it together.

Moreover, I concluded after looking into the mirror in Elmira's bedroom, lodgings that I shared with her full-time now that I'd abandoned the room at the hotel that I never used, that I was not in the best position to handle something descending on Shadow Valley from parts unknown.

I couldn't see myself clearly, but what I could see didn't look all that great. Even though Carmody had washed out my eyes with a cascade of water, the part that used to be white was now streaky and red as a fall sunset. The alcohol-induced euphoria of the night before had surrendered to a reality-induced morning of pain. There were painful bruises on both sides of my head from where Ivey had swatted me with his weird conical skull, and when I tried to look closely at them they sort of spun out of my view. The room was moving, but somehow not moving, at the same time.

And then, just to make the coming day perfect, I heard gunshots.

Chapter 45

I rode out to find the shots. Walking was painful and tedious.

By the time I had ridden about halfway to the clearing at the edge of town, where I reckoned the shots emanated, I employed my crack detective skills to figure out that it had to be someone taking target practice because the shots came six at a time, spaced evenly, interrupted by a pause for a reload.

I was right. It was Bosco, and he was drawing and shooting at a target he'd nailed to a loblolly. It was the same tree where I'd nailed targets and practiced when recovering from a shot to the shoulder last year.

I'd spent days pitifully and theatrically struggling to shoot with my injured right arm, with fence-leaners and passersby – including the gunman Purcell, who was waiting for a chance to draw on me – eyeing my lack of progress.

It wasn't all a show. My right hand didn't work that well back then because of a bullet I'd taken that had scrambled bone and flesh. But I was still suckering Purcell, because when the time came for us to have it out, he was concentrating on my half-dead right arm and didn't notice that I was reaching with my left hand for a pistol I carried in my pocket.

My right arm eventually recovered.

Purcell did not.

Billy Gannon's murder was avenged, but part of the story behind Gannon's death died with Purcell.

Early in my investigation I'd figured out that Purcell had been running a campaign of intimidation against Elmira – scaring away customers and trying to put her out of business – so that Eddie Moon could buy the Silver Spoon. As I noted before, Moon didn't particularly *want* the Spoon, but Purcell had muscled his way into Moon's business so he'd have a discrete way to buy the Spoon at a fire-sale price. So Purcell forced Moon to play along.

Purcell wanted the Spoon, but couldn't have cared less about the bar. He wanted the scrub land in back of the joint, which was in the planned path of a new railroad.

Purcell knew that owning land next to a railroad line is more of a gold mine than an actual gold mine.

I got in Purcell's way, and eventually killed him. And as is so often the case in the futility of gunfighting, after all the shooting was over, it turned out that more strings were pulled and the planned route changed, presumably to someone who could offer a bigger bribe.

Railroad lines were the biggest business going, and the stroke of a pencil line on a map could mean millions. It was a high-stakes game at a lot of levels, including mine, down where the bullets were flying.

Whether Purcell was running the deal solo of if he was put up to it by a higher-level crook was a secret he took to the grave. I know that for a fact because I buried him in that grave. I could see the cemetery from atop the Steeldust if I stood up in the stirrups.

Bosco stopped shooting and holstered his gun.

"There's no law against target shooting," I said, "but you can save me a trip next time if you let me know in advance."

"I'll do that," he said.

"What happened to your hand?" I asked.

It was wrapped in bandages stained by rust-color old blood and some fresh crimson dots.

Bosco regarded it in a detached way, as though it were somebody else's hand.

"Rubbed it a little raw practicing," he said.

"You've only been shooting for a few minutes."

"I've been practicing the action, drawing and dry-firing, for the better part of two days," he said, flexing his fingers. "I started slow, worked up speed, and today's the first day with actual bullets."

"This is the part that counts," I said. "It's good to be quick, but speed doesn't do anything for you if you miss."

Bosco nodded.

"I heard this is where you do your practicing," he said.

I dismounted and walked over to him. I ground-hitched the Steeldust, who was used to gunfire, so I knew he wouldn't spook.

"Why are you doing this?" I asked.

Bosco looked down and fiddled with the cylinder.

"Because I will never be caught defenseless again."

That said it all, and I saw no reason to argue the case, but I did feel the need to point something out to him.

"I understand that," I said. "Completely. But be aware of a couple things. First, being in a gunfight isn't like a magic trick. It's not just a matter of the right physical action. You've got to stand in the face of incoming fire and adapt to a fluid situation. Second, sometimes having a gun, and trying to use it, heightens your risk, escalates the situation."

"Meaning?"

"Meaning that if you carry a gun it makes it more likely somebody who has a gun will use it against you. So my advice is – learn how to use it properly, and if you feel the need to employ a weapon, don't hesitate. Don't take it out of the holster unless you are prepared to use it."

Bosco looked like he was going to say something, but he shrugged and turned back to the tree. He'd tacked a pockmarked bulls-eye target to the loblolly, and had some beat-up cans lined up on a broad tree stump.

He drew and fired at the target, nicking the edge of the first ring outside the bulls-eye. Then he methodically picked off three cans.

"Excellent," I said. "But don't aim. Point – but don't aim."

"I don't understand what that means," he said.

"It means don't sight down the gun. A pistol is an extension of your hand, not a rifle. Shoot with your elbow at your side, not with the gun out in front of you. Don't do what you're doing now, which is to aim by looking down the…"

Bosco looked at me and I looked at him. I could not think of the word so I took out my pistol and drew my hand along it.

Along the *barrel*.

That was it. *Barrel*. A word that I knew. I *knew* that I knew but my mind was playing hide-and-seek with the word. I've had that happen before with people's names, but how, I wondered, could I forget the word for part of my gun.

Bosco seemed as puzzled as I was but he's not the type to lose his composure just because I was losing mine.

So he asked me to demonstrate.

I retrieved the cans and set two of them on the stump and one on the ground about sixty feet away.

"Don't straighten your knees," I told Bosco. "Stay light. And be sure you look directly at what you intend to shoot."

I followed my own advice and I noticed that the bull's eye momentary split into two parts and fused itself again. Taking advantage of the split-second when it became one in my vision, I drew and pulled the trigger as my hand rose and I leaned back and I hit the target dead-center. My gun barrel – yes, that *was* the word, the *barrel* – was no more than in inch above and two six inches in front of the holster.

"*Shit*," Bosco said. "Son of a *bitch*."

The gunfire was starting to make my head hurt again but not enough to keep me from gloating.

"Imagine your hand is a hundred feet long," I said. "Imagine you're reaching out to touch what you're trying to hit. Keep your forearm level with the ground. Lean back when you shoot. Don't aim. Just *feel*."

Bosco's effort wasn't particularly graceful, but he fired off a good shot, hitting more than half of the edge of the center spot.

He reloaded.

"Now I'll try the cans," he said.

"The ones on the stump are not what you want to concentrate on for now," I said, and Bosco turned toward me. I could almost feel his attention seize me by the shoulders. Bosco was pouring the same intensity into shooting practice that he'd funneled into learning card tricks or memorizing his hundreds of permutations of mind-reading code.

"It's only in the stage-plays," I said, "that people get blown flat on their back with the first hit from a pistol. Sometimes even a shot that's eventually fatal doesn't even slow them down for the first few seconds. When you hit a man he can still shoot back. He can still run, maybe for a short time, but long enough to seek cover or charge you or get a better position to fire on you."

"So what's this have to do with the cans?"

"Bosco, I don't know what you're getting ready for in particular, and in any event I'm not sure I really *want* to know, but whatever it is it's not going to be picking cans off a tree stump. So shoot at the can on the ground, follow its movement when you hit it, shoot it again, and duck and roll and shoot it again."

I admit I liked out-dramatizing Bosco, and while I couldn't compete with his stage presence on a real stage, we were in my theater of operations now. Without any preamble I drew, hit the can, hit it again as it spun in the air, and did a shoulder roll to my right.

I was up on one knee and firing before the can stopped skipping along the grass and I followed it with my remaining three rounds, making it dart and skitter violently every time I hit it.

Bosco stared at me with his mouth open. I couldn't improve on what I'd just done and figured it was time for me to make my exit. But when I started walking away, something in my head went off-kilter and I had a hard time keeping my balance and I moved toward my mount the way a drowning man pursues a life raft.

I made it, and stood there for a second, stabilizing myself by holding onto the thing in the middle of the saddle. The knob that I hold onto if the riding is rough. On the rare occasions when I'm roping something I keep some line looped around the goddamned thing.

The *thing*.

The *pommel*. Yes, the *pommel*.

As soon as I could keep my balance I used the goddamned pommel to hoist myself up and I rode away without saying goodbye.

Chapter 46

"You look like you been rode hard and put away wet," Carmody said, swallowing coffee out of a battered tin cup. The coffee was damn near boiling and I don't know how he could gulp it like that, but Carmody's one of those people who seems impervious to discomfort.

"Thank you," I said.

"You ain't looked in a mirror lately, have you?"

"Just a little," I said.

"Don't blame you. But in addition to your – what should I say? – *cosmetic* issues, the pupils of your eyes is different sizes. That ain't healthy."

"No," I said, "it's not. But it's happened before and I survived. Not in a fight but when I caught a piece of shrapnel in the head."

Carmody leaned back and nodded as though he was basking in the glow of a great revelation.

"So *that's* what happened."

"Can we stick to the subject?" I wasn't annoyed, exactly, but we had the office to ourselves for once and wanted to get down to business.

Swingle was out running errands. He was shopping for *curtains*. For a *cell*.

Carmody spread his hands and shrugged.

"What *is* the subject?"

"I don't know," I admitted.

"My point exactly," Carmody said. "You got hit so hard your brain is coughing up hairballs."

"No, I mean I'm so far in the dark about what's going on here that I don't know where to begin to even try to figure it out."

Carmody turned serious, walked to the stove, poured himself more coffee and brought me a cup.

"I think we're in big trouble," he said, looking into the bottom of the cup, moving the cup in a small circle to make the liquid swirl and staring into it as though he expected to find an answer at the bottom.

"I think so, too," I said. "It's been one damn thing after another and I haven't even had a chance to sit down with you and figure it out."

We sat in silence for a long while. We've known each other long enough so it doesn't bother either of us.

After a while, he cleared his throat.

"I ain't figured it out yet," Carmody said. "You?"

"Let's start from the beginning," I said.

Carmody rolled his eyes.

"You ain't gonna start counting things off on your fingers, is you?"

"First," I said, holding out the index finger of my left hand and touching it with the index finger of my right, bending it back a little, "this all started when I got that letter from Gus Marner. He didn't tell me much, but he said there were strange things going on and he didn't know why. Before the letter reaches me, he shoots himself. Or at least he's found dead with a gun in his hand."

"And they don't have no local marshal," Carmody said, "to stick pencils in the dead man's head and figure it was murder."

"Second," I said, holding up another finger, "we find marked cards in the Spoon. The guy who was winning at the time was probably reading them, but we'll never know for sure because Swingle killed him."

Carmody was staring at my fingers and I knew that my habit grated him all red-assed. I savored the moment despite my headache.

"My guess," Carmody said, "is that he was reading the cards. And that whoever had pawned off the marked cards on the distributor cut other people in on the deal. I've heard of that racket before. You plant the cards in advance and then you've got a group of sharpies who move from place to place, and of course they win big. And as tribute, they kick back a share of the winnings to the person who planted the cards."

"I've heard of that, too," I said, "but something about this bothers me. Bosco checked, and *all* the decks we'd bought were marked. All twenty."

"I know that," Carmody said. "So?"

"Bosco mentioned to me later – maybe you weren't there – that it's not the way it's usually done. Usually just one or two decks are in circulation and the sharpies keep an eye out and join the game when they see the marked cards. Marking all the decks makes the odds of detection too high. Bosco said that he'd noticed right away because that's his business, but experienced card players would have caught on soon enough if *every* deck they played with was marked."

"You're saying somebody wanted to stir things up here?"

"No," I said, "I'm not saying that for sure, and neither did Bosco. It's just a possibility."

Carmody gave me a speed-up gesture and told me to get on to finger number three.

"Third," I said, holding up three fingers and watching Carmody wince, "a bunch of thugs ride into town with the intent of roughing me up and busting up the Spoon. And they make it a point to separate me from the bar by luring me, and maybe luring you, too, up into the hills."

"You're saying they baited us?" Carmody said.

"Yes, exactly. It was too easy to spot them. Normally, that's the way a bunch of hired goons who weren't used to woodsmanship would make their way down a trail."

"So?" Carmody asked.

"So the guy who led them in knew better. I saw him hug the tree line out of habit and rein his mount away from a broad, bare section where he'd leave tracks. He didn't do it on purpose, just out of habit. The way a careful man moves after years of practice."

"But then," Carmody said, "he exposed himself on purpose."

"Yes. He rode out right into the open. If he really wanted to sneak into town he could have. But he let his bumpkin brigade be noticed and we came to him – just like dogs called to dinner."

Carmody set his cup down carefully and I could see the realization in his eyes as clearly as he could probably see it in mine, even though my eyes were currently of oddball sizes.

"But then, the plan went to hell when your insane little friend started blasting," he said. "They never expected that ferocity of resistance."

"General Lee never expected that ferocity of resistance," I said.

Carmody leaned forward.

"Maybe the ones who was going to stage the brawl was also expecting to conveniently find the marked decks and really make trouble for us," he said.

"Plausible," I said.

I knew I almost had Carmody's goat and took my time holding up four fingers.

"Fourth, having failed to get me out of the way, they rustle up a prizefighter to beat hell out of me. They didn't have a lot of time, but there are plenty of fighters around and whoever was behind this knew I'd been a fighter myself but probably assumed I'd be easy pickings."

"Because of your age, and general deterioration," Carmody said.

I didn't take his bait.

"And then in the midst of all this – "

"I sense a thumb in my future," Carmody said.

"And then I start counting on the other hand," I said. "There's more."

Carmody just looked at me.

"Fifth," I said, "our liquor supply is busted up.

"Sixth, Bosco tries to find out what happened in New Paradise and gets roughed up and Gina is abused.

"Seventh, Eddie Moon turns up dead, maybe because he was getting pressured, too, and didn't want to play along.

"Eighth, whoever is behind this digs up a real fighter and tries to put me out of action for good. You can't just murder a town marshal. Even out here in our little stretch of hell, that would draw too much attention from the law. But rough him up so bad he has to slink out of town, or maybe beat him to death in the process? In a fair match between two experienced prizefighters? That wouldn't even make the paper, even if we had one."

"Dead Horse Hill might send a reporter to cover it," Carmody said.

"On a slow day," I agreed.

Carmody rubbed his wiry beard, and it made a sound like a brush on a hardwood floor.

"So what do we do?" he said.

"We go into full battle mode," I said. "We get together everybody here we can depend on – Miller, Oak, Bosco, and Swingle – and put them on alert."

"You think we can trust Bosco and Swingle? How do we know they ain't part of what's going on?"

"I thought about that," I said. "And checked. It turns out Elmira approached Bosco, not the other way around, contacting him through a booking agent. Bosco didn't come to her. Now, somebody could have gotten to him in the interim, and re-cruited him to be part of the plan, but that's not likely."

"Agreed," Carmody said. "How about your rabid little pet weasel? After all, he did the shooting that kicked off this whole business."

"He's popped in and out of my life for more than ten years," I said. "Usually to remind me that he saved my life and then to cause some random trouble and get me to mop up after him. Swingle's mean and crazy, but he's also insanely loyal."

"Had a dog like that once," Carmody said.

And then we were comfortably silent for a few minutes.

"You know, we ain't no further ahead in figuring out who done this," Carmody said. "We know it's somebody who's got it in for you personal, and seems to want to mess with the Spoon, Eddie Moon's place, and maybe Gus Marner's, but we don't even know why, much less who."

"I think we have to go to New Paradise," I said. "As much as I hate to leave things vulnerable here, that's where the thread began to unravel and we need to go pull on it."

Carmody drummed his fingers on the table.

"We got no jurisdiction in New Paradise," he said. "Maybe you should call in some of your buddies in the state."

"And tell them what?" I said. "Some far-fetched conspiracy theory? That's how they'd look at it, and I don't blame them. And if we cry wolf, it could make things tough when we do need them."

"Well," Carmody said, "we could dig up Moon and stick more pencils in his head. That would convince them for sure."

I laughed in spite of myself.

"We need to handle this ourselves," I said. "But I need to stay here. You need to back up Bosco. We have no idea what might happen and he's not up to defending himself yet. And I'm not sure he'd know what to look for. But he's tough and clever. You two will make a good pair."

"If there's serious shit coming down here," Carmody said, "you can't handle it yourself, especially with the condition you're in."

"I've got Swingle," I said.

"And he's worth two men," Carmody said, "but I think you better call in Taza."

Taza is Elmira's son-in-law. Well, sort of. He's an Apache, and is possibly married to Elmira's daughter. We never quite figured out how the relationship translates from one culture and legal system to another.

"Taza still says he plans to kill me," I said.

"But he wants to take his time doing it, so he's got a vested interest in keeping you alive in the short run. I say we call him out. He can bring in more men. He's the closest thing to the cavalry we've got."

"Let's do it," I said. "Quick. God knows what else is going to happen."

"What the hell else *could* happen?" Carmody said.

Just then the door flew open and slammed against the wall. Carmody and I jumped straight up like jack-in-the-boxes.

It was Elmira. I'd asked her to stop barging into rooms like that because some day she's going to get shot. But she's excitable and can't help herself.

She was panting from the run over.

"You won't believe what just happened," she said.

Chapter 47

She held the damn poster in her hand, and she was right.

I couldn't believe it. I actually rubbed my raw eyes and looked again. It was still there, in big, black, bold letters.

"You didn't tell me nothing about this," Carmody said.

"It's the first I've seen it," I said. "First I've heard of it."

"Are you crazy?" Elmira said. Her voice was shaky, and she looked ready to launch into one of her crying jags.

Carmody shook his head.

"You is nuttier than a squirrel turd," he said.

"Where'd this come from?" I asked Elmira.

"Bassett, the guy who managed that bald fighter you tried to kill."

"I didn't try to – wait, Bassett's *here? Now?* Nailing these up?"

He just rode out of town," Elmira said. "The trail by the bank, where you tried to kill the bald guy. You can probably catch up to him and back out of this before you wind up like that bald guy, making sheep noises and drooling on yourself."

I was out the door in a second but came back to grab the poster. I couldn't help taking another look at it.

"The drawing looks just like you," Carmody said. "Except they made your hair darker. Got rid of the gray."

Elmira, who is easily distracted, forgot her current state of panic and looked at me, the poster, and me again.

"It actually takes ten years off you," she said.

I said a word I don't usually say in front of her and left again. But not before I took another look at the poster.

I couldn't help it. I didn't want to, but I couldn't stop. It's like when you have a sore tooth and can't keep yourself from touching it with your tongue.

Bassett had a good memory for faces or the artist was good at recreating likenesses, or both. It did look just like me, the drawing of me squaring off with a lean, muscular man with glossy hair parted in the middle, who stared back at me from the right side of the poster, his fists upraised in a posture mimicking mine.

In the center of the poster, in ornate black capitals, were the words I still could not comprehend:

DEFENDING CHAMPION
JOHN STOKES
VS.

CHALLENGER
JOSIAH HAWKE
FOR THE UNDISPUTED
HEAVYWEIGHT CHAMPIONSHIP OF THE
WEST
OCT 22, 1877
4 PM AT THE SHADOW VALLEY AMPHI-
THEATER

Chapter 48

Bassett tried to outrun me, but he could tell it was futile. My Steeldust was bred for speed, and over a quarter mile it's pretty much as fast as any thoroughbred.

I also shouted that I'd shoot him if he didn't stop, and he wasn't sure I was bluffing. I wasn't convinced of it myself, but he couldn't answer my questions if he were dead, so I decided I should hold off on plugging him.

For a while, anyway.

He reined his mount to a halt and put his hands straight up like a man trying to touch the sky with his fingertips.

"It ain't my doing," he said.

"What the hell *is* this?"

"I told Ludd about how you tried to kill Ivey."

"I didn't try to – wait a minute, what does Ludd have to do with it?"

"Ludd damn near had a conniption when I told him what you done to Ivey, and he took off saying The Man ain't gonna like it, and an hour later Ludd came back – all pale and shaky – and told me to set this fight up."

"You got Stokes to agree to this? He's in Austin?"

Bassett shook his head.

"Kansas City. Ludd said there was telegrams exchanged."

"You're telling me that this guy, a champion fighter, agreed to this sight unseen? No contracts? No discussion of the purse?"

"I didn't say that. From what I was told, which weren't much, Stokes was offered a big purse and travel money regardless of whether you showed up or not."

"Did it occur to him, or you, or anybody else to check and see if I would really take this fight?"

"Ludd said that if you chickened out you'd never be able to show your face in town and it would still be worth it."

"*Worth it*? To whom?"

"To *whom*?" Bassett echoed. "You sure talk puffed up for a town marshal in the ass end of nowhere. You stick your pinky out when you drink your tea? To *whom?* To The Man, whoever he is, the guy that's got a hard-on to get you out of his way, that's *whom*."

"I'm supposed to fight for free?"

"Loser gets five hundred dollars. If I was you, I'd show up, eat an easy punch, and take a dive. Easiest money you'll ever make."

"Suppose I win?"

"You ain't gonna win."

"Humor me," I said.

"Winner's share is ten thousand dollars."

I wasn't sure I heard right.

"Ten thousand dollars? Ten *thousand?*"

"Don't even think about it," Bassett said. "That ain't going to happen."

I fished the folded poster out of my pocket, looked at it again, and held it up.

"Where else are you posting these?"

"In Austin and San Antonio," Bassett said. "Ludd's men probably already have them up. Stokes is a big name, and we'll draw a nice crowd even if it is a day's ride or more to this place. And if you show some common sense and disappear, we can find plenty of real fighters willing to substitute. Hell, *I'd* take a beating for five hundred dollars."

I was reaching the end of my tether.

"Damn it, Bassett, can I bring you back to reality and remind you that there is no 'Shadow Valley Amphitheater?' We have a theater that doubles as a church and holds a hundred people at most and you wouldn't have room for a cockfight on the stage."

Bassett jerked his thumb back the way he'd ridden.

"I may be a little extravagant with my words," he said, "but the clearing where you tried to kill Ivey is as good as any outdoor spot."

I let it pass.

"I've set up lots of big fights in places worse than that," Bassett said. You've got a wide road and a steep hill on one side. We can nail together long benches thirty or forty feet up the hill and fashion maybe a hundred chairs ringside all around the circle and you've got an amphitheater. And it'll be easy to charge the spectators because there's only two ways in and out – where the road narrows on either side of the clearing."

"Bassett," I said, hearing the exasperation in my voice that I could no longer disguise, "suppose I just don't go along with this? Not only don't I have to show up, I can just forbid you setting up a fight on a town road."

Bassett turned somber and, to my eye, a little embarrassed.

"You can do that," he said. "But I've got a feeling it'll wind up in the papers as 'local marshal chickens out of fight and uses loophole as excuse.'"

And then he suddenly spoke up with anger.

"Damn it, this ain't my doing. I'm one checker on a big board and I get pushed around by a finger I can't see. But I promised you that I would keep an ear to the ground and let you know what I heard, and I ain't heard much but I'm telling you all I know. And all I damn well know is that the person behind Ludd is willing to pony up ten thousand dollars to get you out of the way."

I had a feeling there was more, so I waited him out.

"I heard Ludd talking to one of his henchmen, and sort of nosed in on the conversation. Ludd said they'll win either way. If you chicken out or get the crap beat out of you, you're '*discredited and no longer an obstacle.'* That's how he put it: *'discredited and no longer an obstacle.'* Guy talks more sissified than you."

I nodded and waited some more.

"And if you get killed," Bassett said, "which you have a good chance of doing if you get in the ring against Stokes, so much the better."

"So much the better," I repeated.

"And even though The Man is fronting all that money, Ludd says it's worth it because he might make it back, from admissions the day of and from what he called 'profits in the long run.'"

"What's that mean, do you think, 'profits in the long run?'"

"I do not know," Bassett said, in an oddly formal way, shaking his head and biting his lower lip. "Except for one thing he said that sounded real strange."

"What did he say?

"He said all this would pay for itself after we 'moved in.'"

"Moved in?"

"*Moved in.* That's all I know. I didn't want to push and spook him. Ludd gets the idea I'm pumping him for information I'll wind up dead for sure."

"Thanks, Bassett," I said, sensing that the well was dry and there was no sense in cranking the pump any more.

We both shrugged and I told him to be on his way.

But before we turned tails I asked him if he had any idea, even a guess, maybe an unrelated clue, about the identity of this person who wanted me out of the way so badly.

"I don't know who," Bassett said, reigning the horse in a circle.

And then he shouted over his shoulder.

"And I don't know *whom,* neither, your Royal Majesty," he said and spurred his mount to a gallop.

Chapter 49

I told Carmody to set up an emergency council of war.

As I said it, it occurred to me that maybe Bassett was right and I was getting a little puffed up in my words, because what I was really asking was for Carmody to round up my only friends, which was a pitifully small group that could fit comfortably around the table in Elmira's back office.

And for the record, calling them "friends" was pushing it. One of them – Bosco – I didn't really know that well, and another – Taza – had threatened to murder me.

Actually, he threatened that he would torture me until I begged him to let me die. I guess there's a subtle difference.

But you take help where you can get it, and right how I needed help.

They were all looking at me, waiting for me to begin. I looked at each of them individually, moving my gaze clockwise around the table.

There was something sinister bearing down on us, I was sure of it, even though I didn't know what. The prizefight was a minor, but bizarre, part of the puzzle. We were dealing with two murders, if you assumed Marner's death was staged as a suicide, an orchestrated attack on the Spoon and its liquor supplier, and vague inferences from Bassett that powerful forces were arrayed against us.

I needed to convince everyone at the table that we were facing what in a former life I would have called an existential problem, and figure out how their skills could play into our defense.

To my left was Carmody. The best woodsman and tracker I'd ever known, a crack rifle shot, and someone who knew my moves as well as I knew his. When we fought together we had an effectiveness that was more than the sum of the parts. An adversary faced more than Hawke plus Carmody. It was more like Hawke *multiplied* by Carmody.

Then there was Bosco. I sensed in him a deep well of resourcefulness, but more importantly a white-hot rage against whoever and whatever was behind the attack on him and Gina.

Next, I fixed my gaze on Vern Miller, the taciturn druggist. I'd known him since I came to Shadow Valley but I never actually knew much about his background. He was a human clam when it came to talking about his past, but once he'd let it slip that he'd been a captain in the war and I believe he'd seen action before that, based on the fact that the first time he came to my defense he was using an antique flintlock, probably plucked from his fireplace mantel. Miller was a dour and mysterious man, somewhere between 60 and 110 years old. He had shown himself to be fearless under fire and a master battle strategist when we orchestrated a rescue mission last year. I'm not sure what happened to Miller during the war but he once told me had had his fill of gunplay and violence and regretted the fact that he was so goddamned good at it that he kept getting drawn back into one sort of battle after another.

Miller touched shoulders with the man next to him, Richard Oak, the blacksmith. Oak's shoulders took up about twice the space of a normal man's, and the leathery skin of his forearms was stretched tightly over muscles and veins that looked like intertwined cables and tree branches. He'd seen limited action during the war, which was lucky for him. I could tell from the first time that he rushed to my defense with what was basically a toy popgun, bless his heart, and stood, confused, in the middle of the street making a target of himself, that he was a totally inept gunfighter. But he knew no fear and had an innate sense of decency.

Elmira was leaning against Oak's other shoulder. She was the toughest person in the room. Not physically, of course, and she'd never shot a gun – maybe never even *touched* one – but she'd weathered hard times that would have crippled a normal person, man or woman, and had some innate, instinctive way of rallying folks when they are down.

Then there was Swingle, who had popped in and out of my life for a decade. Yes, the rabid little weasel was certifiable and in terms of homicide he probably had the highest body count of anybody in the room. But some men are born for battle. I don't mean that they're necessarily master strategists, although Swingle probably understood tactics and plans as well as anyone. For Swingle and his species, death and destruction are the air they breathe.

Taza arrived late and sat in the last chair, elbowing me in as he lowered himself. He was tall for an Indian, probably about six-three, and was broad and powerful and, I knew from frightening experience, even stronger than he looked. Taza and I had met under less than cordial circumstances, when Carmody goaded him into a mano-a-mano knife fight with me after we'd been captured by Taza's Apache scouting party.

Carmody, who speaks enough of their language to convey every profane phrase in their vocabulary, told Taza I had insulted him, provided explicit details of my imagined affronts against Taza, and suggested that instead of just killing us, Taza be a sport about it and duel to the death, letting us go if I won. It had not gone particularly well for me until I chopped Taza down with a leg kick and he fell forward, accidentally impaling himself on his own knife.

Taza lived up to his end of the bargain and later saved me from a Comanche attack, making it clear that he saved my life only to preserve the delicious opportunity for him to kill me slowly some day in the future.

"I am sorry," Taza said in that formal monotone of his, scraping his chair forward. He speaks English better than most cowhands but hid that fact from me during our initial confrontation.

"I did not mean to poke you as I sat down," he said, dragging the chair forward once again and nudging me with the same elbow.

"Please do not throw one of your tantrums and kick me in shin like angry little girl," he said.

As I was asking him for help, and needed it, I had no alternative but to absorb whatever he chose to dish out.

***

Over the next quarter-hour, I laid out the situation in detail. I told them all how my instincts were telling me this was a coordinated effort to take over the bar, maybe both bars in town, and maybe bars within a large radius – if Marner's situation was part of the plot.

I looked at Elmira and gently told her something that had only recently occurred to me. I didn't want to say it but had to.

There could be a threat to her safety, too, given what happened to Moon and Marner.

She nodded and tried not to look frightened.

I continued, explaining that someone was clearly intent on getting me out of the way, but doing so in a manner that would not provoke further involvement from law enforcement.

And I told them that this fight nonsense was the latest wrinkle in an effort by somebody with bushels of money and tons of hatred for yours truly.

Then I asked them what they thought.

I was hoping for some insight. Maybe scraps of information we could link together to form a comprehensible chain of events. Or plans for how we could keep Shadow Valley safe while we investigated what happened to Gus Marner in New Paradise. Or whether other bars within a 30-mile radius had encountered similar problems.

Or something.

Anything.

I asked, again, what they thought.

"What do I think?" Miller said, his pickle-sucking expression adding gravity to the rhetorical question he floated.

"I think," he said, "you're going to get knocked out inside two rounds."

Chapter 50

I never really regained control of the situation after that.

Twenty minutes later, Carmody had written all the bets and the odds on the back of some butcher paper Elmira kept in the store room. It was complicated because nobody was placing straight win-lose bets, because everybody – except Carmody, who said he intended to referee and thus couldn't not be seen as beholden to an outcome, and Taza, who said he would reserve judgment – assumed I would lose.

Elmira said I had no chance and she was afraid I'd be badly hurt and asked me not to fight and started to cry, one of those jags she has where she runs short of air. But when she caught her breath she reminded everyone that since the bets were being placed in her gambling establishment the house gets a cut.

Anyway, the betting was primarily on the round in which I would be knocked out.

But that was complicated too, because no one had mentioned the rules under which the bout would be fought. Most events out our way were contested with some version of the London Prize Rules, under which rounds lasted until a knockdown and then there was a 30-second rest period. But in some of the big cities they'd started using three-minute timed rounds with a one-minute rest period.

So Carmody took bets under both sets of circumstances. Generally, I was predicted to go in the first round under timed rounds, longer under the London rules because it was common for a fighter to go down on purpose to prolong the inevitable.

I've been told that the real London rules, which are written down somewhere, presumably in London, prohibit grappling and kicking. Very few bareknuckle events are actually fought that way, but some are, and the betting ran even more heavily against me if it was fists only.

I kept my temper until they started placing bets on how many teeth I would lose.

I brought my fist down on the table so hard that I put a crack in the thick oak.

It's not like me to lose my temper like that, even with provocation, and God knows I get enough of it, and they all stared at me, startled by the sudden violence and that crazy crackling sound my hand emitted again.

If it were possible for me to stare at myself I would have, such was my shock at my action, but all I could do is look at my fist and the cleavage in the table.

Maybe Carmody was right. Something in my head had gotten scrambled by that bald battering ram. I'd seen this before in punch-drunk old fighters, the hair-trigger explosion, followed by disbelief and remorse.

"Sorry, I said, and looked at my hand again. I flexed it. It still made that crazy snapping and popping sound, but it didn't hurt much, even though I'd slammed it full-force into three inches of heavy wood.

Taza reached over and pushed at the crack with his index finger. There was a creak and the table buckled in the middle and both halves leaned in on each other and came to rest in my lap.

"What is total pot?" Taza said.

Carmody's mind was elsewhere.

"Huh?"

"How much everyone has bet all together?" Taza said.

Carmody did the math in his head. He can take painful amounts of time responding to normal questions, but when it comes to gambling chits, his mind flashes like heat lightning.

"One hundred twenty-one dollars."

"Then I bet one hundred twenty-one dollars against all of you. Even money. One-hundred twenty-one dollars on the crazy man who breaks tables with his noisy hand. I bet he will win."

Chapter 51

It was Monday, October 15, and I had exactly one week before, as Carmody put it, I would be beat like a rented mule.

I wasn't even sure what that meant and I shrugged it off, as I did the ten thousand or so other euphemisms everybody came up with, colorfully predicting my pulverization. I was, according to friends, enemies, and passersby, to be *hammered, pasted, smeared*, and *smashed*. One cowhand who had an accent I couldn't place said I would be *rumbusticated*, a new word for me, origins unknown. A grizzled geezer, a cook for a passing trail drive, said he'd heard of Stokes and I was going to be *banjoed* for sure.

Somehow, getting *banjoed* seemed the most sinister of all the prophecies, though I'm not sure why.

I had a lot of time to think about my fate because everyone in my circle except Elmira, Swingle, and Taza were out scouting in a 25-mile radius, checking out the larger gambling and drinking spots. We couldn't visit every hole-in-the wall bar, but we could get a sampling of places comparable to the Spoon, The Full Moon, and Gus Marner's.

Carmody and Bosco headed to New Paradise. Bosco noted in a matter-of-fact way that he would not be easy pickings this time around. I wasn't sure if he referred to the fact that he was armed this time, or to the hulking Carmody who was carrying his artillery-size shotgun along with a repeating rifle.

I assured him he was ready this time, but urged caution anyway.

Carmody and Bosco would look into the Marner incident and then head south to Copper Ridge, where they'd check out The Oasis, which was about the size of the Spoon. Carmody had been to Copper Ridge several times, and I had heard of it, but knew very little of The Oasis, not even the name of the owner.

I asked Elmira and she didn't know who owned it, either. I thought it odd that she knew nothing about a competitor a day's ride southwest, but then it occurred to me in this relative wilderness twenty miles was pretty much the same as two hundred or two thousand – a whole other universe.

It's not like my native Illinois where everything is pretty much mapped out and there are passable roads in between population centers of any size.

While Shadow Valley had clear and well-traveled trails to the northeast, leading to Austin, and trails to the far southwest, leading to San Antonio, traveling sideways to the small settlements around us could be an adventure.

Miller and Oak would ride northeast to Bitterweed, where there was a casino called The Sapphire. They'd pick up whatever information he could and then head down to the town of Fort Harmony, where there was, oddly, no fort, but there was a casino. It was called The Palace.

To us, that was the extent of our known universe. There were larger population centers father out, Blanco to the west, Driftwood to the north, San Marcos to the east, and New Braunfels to the south. I'd never been to any of them. There were the major cities of Austin and San Antonio on the next ring distant from our town, and I'd travelled to both of them many times, but we only had so many men and so much time so we stayed local, sticking with places similar in size. In fact, while nobody keeps track of exact population because everybody moves too much to count them, we were a comparative metropolis compared to the towns we were scouting.

After all, we had two casinos.

Taza had rounded up a half-dozen braves to keep watch with me in Shadow Valley. He also sent young men – boys, really – on fast horses to meet Carmody, Bosco, Miller, and Oak on the trails and bring back dispatches to me. That way I could be updated in a timely manner and not have to wait until the men completed their rounds.

But updated about *what?*

What was going on? After all this commotion and I still had nothing concrete other than an ominous gnawing in what was left of my mind that the deaths of Moon and Marner, the deaths of the goons who tried to break up the Spoon, and now this strange fight scenario were somehow part of a series of boxcars hooked to a locomotive that was bearing down on me.

And maybe on Elmira.

Chapter 52

Carmody's dispatch came in Tuesday morning.

I was walking into my office when a young Apache trotted by on a vividly colored Appaloosa that looked like a black horse upon which somebody had spilled a bucket of white paint.

I stepped into the street and the brave held out an envelope. I could tell it was Carmody's florid, oddly ornate John-Hancock-style writing even from twenty feet away.

The brave didn't even slow down or turn his head to look at me, although the horse, being more sociable, did acknowledge me. The young man, dressed in a blue headscarf and a white tunic, just held the envelope at arm's length and I snatched it, and then he kicked the horse to a gallop and was gone.

It still hadn't rained and the dust kicked up by the Appaloosa was stinging my eyes again, so I went into my office and shut the door before I opened the envelope.

I scanned the stiffly formal writing and entertained a random curiosity about why Carmody does not sing or write with much of an accent.

To Marshal Josiah Hawke, from Deputy Tom Carmody,

This dispatch comes to you from New Paradise. We are leaving there now and are on the way to Copper Ridge and I will file again from there.

There has been a shit load of trouble.

First, I can tell you that Marner's place has been taken over by what you call thugs and goons, which is pretty much what you call everybody you don't like, but these are real thugs and goons for sure. I could tell within a couple minutes that the games are rigged and the liquor is watered down. Before I was spotted I asked around town and was told that the folks who took over Marner's are letting people play on credit and also putting money on the street to loan. In addition to loan-sharking they are also using strongarms to collect. I cannot say for sure but there must some opium or something like it in circulation, because I see folks stumbling around like ghosts, their eyes as vacant as yours after that bald fighter shook the dice inside your head.

I wish I could tell you more but I am pressed for time because me and Bosco are being pursued by a bunch of these losers. They figured out who we was after somebody recognized Bosco.

That would not have been so bad but Bosco would not leave easy and then things got worse when he recognized the goon who attacked Gina.

Bosco egged the goon on and they drew. Bosco put three shots in his heart before the other man cleared the holster. I would not have believed it if I did not see it with my own eyes. Anyway, we lit out of there like badgers with their tails on fire.

They are after us now but they are slickers and not up to the job. And Taza's rider said he will lead them on a wild goose chase in the other direction before he loses them and brings this letter to you.

Yours in haste,
Tom Carmody

Chapter 53

Wednesday was an eventful day. Miller's dispatch came in during the morning and Bassett arrived in the afternoon.

The Apache rider tracked me down at the Spoon, while I was again sweeping up the immortal dust. He did not speak but hung around long enough for me to get the idea that he would not refuse a drink. I thought it was a little early and the rider a little young, but I am not one to judge so I poured a whiskey for him and dumped one in my coffee.

He was intrigued so I poured him a cup of coffee and he dumped his whiskey in it.

The letter was from Miller. I'd never seen his writing before but I could pretty much tell that such neat, tiny block letters would not flow from the hand of the brawny blacksmith.

Also, it was written in the verbiage of a military dispatch. I could almost hear the old sourpuss barking it out.

Oct. 16, 1900 hours
Observation of the Sapphire in the town
of Bitterweed

I know nothing of gambling but some of the locals say the dealers here are sharpies and the dice are shaved, which I assume means that the corners are rounded to make it more likely they fall on certain numbers.

The owner of the bar will not talk to me and locals say that while he is still in town he keeps to himself, mostly staying in his rooms, and when he does appear he looks scared.

I am glad I have Oak with me as escort. The staff at the Sapphire put hands to me when I asked a few questions but backed off when Oak puffed up like a bull.

We strategically retreated before I could find out what was going on in the back room. The entrance was guarded and there was brisk traffic in and out but nobody around here is talkative.

So as not to draw attention, we hid our weapons before riding into town and are picking them up now before riding south. I am half-tempted to take this German bolt-action you gave me and go back and perforate everybody in that miserable hamlet, but I will save that for another day.

More tomorrow.

Respectfully,

Vernon Miller

Basset arrived after lunch. He turned my office chair around and straddled it, leaned on my desk, and went over the rules.

They were pretty standard – as standard as things get in a profession where rules are more like general guidelines and are usually forgotten as soon as the first punch is thrown.

Kicking was all right. Stomping was not. Hitting a downed man was illegal and could result in disqualification. But we both knew that disqualification was an option generally used only when you really wanted a riot and gunshots fired into the ring, so we didn't take that eventuality seriously.

And there would be an actual ring this time. Bassett would set up a 24-footer with three ropes.

That was fine with me. That's a fairly big ring and I move pretty quickly and I figured I'll need all the running room I can get.

Fighters would hold up their open hands at the beginning of each round, turn them palm in and then palm out so that the referee and opponent could see that nothing – including dirt – was being concealed. Rounds would continue until a man hit the ground or went to a knee and the fight would continue until one fighter could not come up to scratch or surrendered from his corner. There would be no fighters' seconds in the ring, although someone could hand the fighter a stool, and only the fighter could surrender.

Bassett had no objection to Carmody refereeing. Referees don't have much authority and should they try to exercise it they are generally subjected to more violence than both of the fighters put together. So it's not exactly a coveted position.

Bassett added a condition, however: Carmody could referee if Bassett held the money.

I said yes.

The fight time couldn't be changed or negotiated because the posters had been printed, but it would probably assure a good crowd, Bassett assured me. Four is late enough so that most working people can knock off and cowhands can break for dinner, but early enough that we would have a good hour-and-a-half before the sun started to go down. That's about an hour longer than most of these matches last. And Mondays are good for drawing migrants and drifters because, unlike on weekends where people are in transit, everybody's pretty much got where they're going to stay for a few days on Monday.

It all sounded good to me, I said.

We sat there with nothing else to talk about but Bassett seemed to want to linger.

That was fine with me because I had nothing else to do except wait for more dispatches and rub my aching temples and try to figure out what the hell was going on. I'd stayed on good terms with Bassett and didn't mind his presence, even though he was complicit in my present predicament. But I knew that he was operating under duress. Also, on occasion Bassett had been less of a jerk than he could have been, which is more than I can say for most people I encounter in my line of work.

I'm not one to get badge-heavy and refuse to talk to people because I consider them low-lifes. You get your best information from people who operate on the sketchy side of the law. I'm in the business of solving, preventing, and avenging crime – and I can't pick up much in the way of useful scuttlebutt from schoolteachers and clergy.

I poured Bassett some coffee even though he didn't ask for it and sat back in my chair.

And then he told me what I needed to know.

Chapter 54

Bassett looked around the room before talking.

Swingle was patrolling the town border, and Carmody was probably in Fort Harmony by now. There was clearly no one else in my tiny little office. But Bassett couldn't help looking around.

It was habit. Habit born of a lifetime of secret-keeping and secret-sharing and secret deal-making and more secretive deal-breaking.

"You know," he said, staring into his cup, "for a lawman you ain't such an asshole."

"Thank you," I said.

"No," Bassett said, "I'm serious. You sweated us some keeping us sardined in that cell, but you could have done worse. The crazy little guy with the mustache said you was the only thing stopping him from working on us with a branding iron. Your lady friend fixed up Ivey best as he'll ever get fixed, and she fed us good. And you could have found a reason to lose me somewhere in a Mexican jail or shoot me 'cause you said I was escaping, and I wouldn't have blamed you one bit. I came here twice with the intention of having my fighter hurt you permanent."

"Three times," I said. "This is number three."

"Yeah," Bassett agreed. "About that…"

I poured some more coffee even though I didn't want it.

"About this fight. You ready to listen to me for a few minutes?"

I nodded.

"And you promise none of this goes outside the room?"

I walked over and threw the lock on the door, more forcefully than I needed to. Elmira and Swingle were the only ones in town who ever just stopped in to the office, but Bassett didn't know that. And a little dramatic reinforcement never hurts.

Bassett glanced around the clearly empty room once more and plucked an envelope from his inside pocket.

"You asked me to find out who was behind all this," he said. "Here's your answer. I heard Ludd talking to one of his henchmen and he said he had to go meet The Man. So I followed him. Row of real fancy houses. Got the mailboxes hung up on the front, right next to the door. Must be nice to be rich – don't even need to walk to the street to get your mail."

Bassett hesitated. I kept him talking with a non-threatening question.

"You walked right up to the door and took the mail?"

"Nope. The mailman had dropped a letter and what with this wind it blew half a block. I saw it and scooped it up. No one noticed nothing."

Bassett then made up his mind.

"Here it is," he said, slapping it down on the desk.

"Now you know why they call him 'The Man.'"

Chapter 55

"*Putz-a-weasel?*" Elmira said, holding the letter in both hands while she lay propped up against the pillow.

"Could be," I said. "Could be anything."

The Man's name was Gregor Pszczystese-wuszył. The mail was a bill for a felted beaver top hat, which told me that he had plenty of money, because the thing cost $40, about two week's wages for a cowhand. Also, I assumed he was not a young man because you hardly see that style of hat worn by anybody under 50.

"Could he be from Poland?"

I shrugged.

"Poland, Bohemia, Moravia, Slovakia," I said. "Maybe the moon."

"*Prick-da-whistle?*" she said.

"Could be," I said, and went to sleep.

Chapter 56

The same young rider was waiting for me, and waiting for his whiskey and coffee, when I came downstairs in the morning. He tapped on the front window and I saw him looking in at me.

He had brought a friend. His friend wanted whiskey and coffee, too.

The riders each put an envelope on the bar. I surmised they had come from opposite directions, and waited for an indeterminate time until I made an appearance. Apaches are so formidable, in part, because of their patience.

Waiting is sometimes the hardest part of any battle. I knew that from the war, and that same itchy feeling, the stress of waiting for something ominous, was coming back to me.

I spread the letters out on the bar and had a whiskey and coffee, too. I opened the one with the flamboyant, baroque handwriting first.

> *Josiah – this ought to reach you Thursday morning. We struck out at Copper Ridge. Didn't get within five miles of the place when we was beset by riders who was obviously lying in wait for us. They must have sent a rider from*

New Paradise right after we skedaddled from there. Bosco and I lost the pursuit, though. Bosco is not a bad rider for somebody from New Jersey. Unlike you he has a sense of direction and keeps his eyes open. We doubled back and found Tarak. That's the 14-year-old boy you are serving whiskey and coffee. Anyway, Bosco and me will go in circles for a while to make sure nobody catches up to us, and then camp for the night and should be back late Thursday.

Yours,
Tom

And then I read the one in the cramped, machine-like printing.

Oct. 17, 22:00
Failure of Mission to Fort Harmony.
I scouted from a high perch and saw riders waiting along the trail we would use to get to Fort Harmony.
I observed them through my high-powered glass and saw no identifying information but did note that they are not experienced at this type of action and knew little about riding. Many were dressed in city clothes and they gripped the reins too tight, held their knees too high and looked at the horses instead of the terrain while riding through rough parts. They

look like they would be more comfortable fighting in an alley than on horseback.

Sorry I cannot be of more help. Oak and I expect to return Thursday.

Respectfully,
Vernon Miller

Chapter 57

Carmody put an elbow on the piano while I played.

It was slow for a Friday night and we had no fights to break up so I went through my repertoire of popular songs. Or at least songs that were popular last time I'd checked.

"You're playing *Alabama Blossoms*," Carmody said.

"That's right."

"Don't that hand hurt you? I can hear them knuckles crack every time you spread your fingers out."

"It doesn't hurt a bit," I said. "Just like when you crack your knuckles, just a lot of noise. I must have knocked something loose when I hit that first kid Bassett sicced on me. I've had this before. A doctor told me it was air in the joints."

"How in hell can you get air blowing in the joints of your hand?"

"I don't know," I said, as I finished an arpeggio and hit the top C on the keyboard, which produced a tinny clink and another knuckle crack.

The piano was wearing out and so was I.

"You know," Carmody said, "you can go through with this fight, like I know you is going to against all common sense, and not got killed."

It came out *git kilt.*

I switched to an up-tempo ballad and played a little louder.

"You don't need to drown me out," Carmody said. "I ain't saying take a dive. I'm just saying that maybe you might not find it necessary to keep getting up if you know you can't win. I know you. You'll keep dragging yourself out of the dirt to get knocked down again."

I held down the sustain pedal on the piano, the one farthest to the right. It doesn't actually make the piano louder but it holds sounds out longer and fills in the gaps between the notes.

"Elmira's scared," Carmody said.

"She's lived through a dozen gunfights," I said.

"But they would have just ended with you *dead.*"

It came out *daaaiiiiid* and he held it longer and louder than I felt necessary.

Carmody could rise above any surrounding noise. It was like he had his own sustain pedal.

"Meaning what?"

"Meaning she's afraid of you winding up like a lot of the pugs you and I know. She don't want to be with a man who drools on himself and flies off the handle for no reason."

I stopped playing and started to stand up.

And then I stopped myself.

Carmody stiffened and lifted his head, ready for me to come at him.

I thought about the one and only time we'd fought. I had been dragged into it reluctantly, trying to keep him from a gunfight he had no chance of surviving, a confrontation with a gunfighter named Henry Best.

Best was every bit as good as Purcell and he wasn't easy to kill, either, but eventually I killed him, too, after Carmody was incapacitated.

At the time, Carmody was determined to defend his honor, even if it meant suicide.

Carmody was much stronger that I was, and I was trying to fight him without hitting him in a potentially fatal way, and as a result, I was losing badly. Carmody had picked me up and was about ready to bull me through a wall when Elmira bopped him on the head with a candlestick.

Carmody's girlfriend had taken the rap, telling Carmody she didn't want to lose him and couldn't help herself because the thought of life without him made her crazy. Carmody saw the logic in that and couldn't stay mad at her for long. Elmira was happy to deflect the blame.

So we'd handcuffed the unconscious Carmody to the brass bar rail while I shot it out with Best and out-drew him, but not by much.

I smoothed my pants and sat back at the bench.

Carmody gets to me from time to time but I'd never gone after him like that. Maybe he was right. Maybe Elmira was right. Something was coming loose in my head.

Carmody shrugged and walked away.

Chapter 58

Bassett and a couple roustabouts came into town and set up the ring on Saturday.

I protested that the ring blocked traffic but Bassett said there was plenty of room to maneuver around it, though the road would have be closed during the fight. And anybody who didn't bother to turn around would be charged admission. And there was no traffic here, anyway.

He also pointed out that I was getting a share of the pot so I should leave him alone and I told him that made sense in sort of a twisted, predatory way.

Bassett took some boards off his wagon and started nailing together benches on the hill. He gave me the head toss that means come along.

When we got near the top of the hill he looked around again, afraid, I suppose, that the mosquitoes would eavesdrop.

"What's The Man got against you?" he said, keeping his eyes on his work.

"You mean...how do you say his name?"

"How the hell do I know? All I know is that I snooped on Ludd again and he said The Man is doing this for two reasons. One is to move in on the territory. The other is to get back at you for what you done."

"What's he after here?" I asked, swatting at a swarm of bugs who were obsessed with my eyeballs. "Why does he want to move in on Shadow Valley?"

Bassett shook his head.

"I don't know for sure," he said, "but for Christ's sake, he's a *criminal*. Figure it out for yourself. Why do criminals move in on anything? To get control, to put their own men in place, to get things for themselves. Smart criminals get organized. They make people buy stuff from one supplier and pay more for it. They make the games crooked and bribe the folks in power to look the other way. They lend money at five times the going rate and break your leg if you don't steal enough to pay it off. They do all the crooked shit they want."

It made sense. I told Bassett he'd make a good law enforcement officer and he flashed me a look of disgust. He swatted at some bugs in front of his mouth and spit and said nothing.

"But what did I allegedly do the guy you call 'The Man?'"

"You mean you don't know?"

"No," I said, and I could feel the anger rising and took a step toward him. "What the hell *did* I do?"

Bassett held up hands.

"I didn't mean it that way. I was just asking the question straight. I wasn't trying to imply that you should know. I was just surprised that he'd get so worked up over something and you wouldn't know what it was."

My hair-trigger temper had almost made Bassett clam up, so I took a minute to take a deep breath and told him I was sorry. I was just on edge.

"Can you find out why he's so mad at me?"

Bassett didn't answer right away.

"I've gone as far as I can. These people are capable of anything."

"So am I," I said, and immediately regretted how stupid I sounded.

"No, you ain't. You draw lines."

"I draw lines?"

"You draw lines," Bassett repeated, as though that said it all. Maybe it did.

He worked in silence for a minute. He was good at hammering the benches together. He'd finished three during the time we'd talked.

"You know," Bassett said, "I did you a good turn in repayment for you not being an asshole, but we ain't friends. When it comes to this fight, I'm in it to see that that Stokes wins and makes Ludd happy and makes The Man happy so I get left alone."

"I understand that."

"Then understand this," Bassett said, turning to me and dropping the hammer. "Stokes is for *real*. That's a real title he has and there's even been talk of him fighting Jem Mace, the world champ. Mace is from England, but he's been living over here and he's looking for opponents and word has it Mace ducked Stokes. If Jem Mace is worried, maybe you should be, too."

"Not much I can do about it now," I said. "You've pretty much got me cornered."

"The Man wants you taught a lesson. That's all I know. And he wouldn't mind too awful much if you wound up dead or mangled in the process. In fact, I think that's the idea."

Bassett picked up the hammer and fitted two boards together and took a second to regain his composure.

"If you get beat bad," he said, "I can't guarantee that'll stop The Man from coming after you, but it can't hurt. No one will think less of you if you stay down the first time you're walloped. Just keep your damned eyes shut and pretend you're asleep."

"Everyone gives me that advice," I said.

"Maybe you should take it. You think your pretty girlfriend wants to see your head scrambled?"

I told him that Elmira swore that she would never watch the fight. She planned on staying holed up in the Spoon and letting Carmody tell her when it was over.

"That woman loves you," Bassett said. "I can see in the way she looks at you. I had a woman once who looked at me that way. She died of the typhoid. I was fighting back then myself. I wasn't in Stokes' league, or yours, but I was doing all right. I gave up fighting when she asked me to. Right before she died. She reminded me I had a daughter to look after. Don't you got nobody to look after?"

The question took me by surprise.

I thought about it for a minute and said yes, but not in the same way.

Bassett pounded in a nail more forcefully than necessary and it occurred to me he was more angry than seemed warranted, and I didn't know why.

"Just remember," Bassett said, "I respect you and thank you for treating me fair. But I ain't your friend."

I nodded.

"I can't be," he said, and walked wordlessly up to the next rise in the hill, carrying his lumber with him.

Chapter 59

Elmira and I went to bed early Sunday night. I wanted to get a good night's sleep, which of course made endless nocturnal conversation irresistible to Elmira.

She asked me again why *pecker-whistle*, as she'd taken to calling him, was so dead-set on seeing me dead, and I again told her I had no answer.

With a suddenness that startled me, she swung a leg over and straddled me, putting her palms on my shoulders and leaning over me, her face no more than a foot away from mine and those astonishingly blue eyes drilling me.

"You don't have anything to prove," she said. "Think about yourself."

"I'm thinking about you," I said.

"Me? What the hell do I care?"

I raised myself on my elbows and she almost toppled off the foot of the bed, catching herself and raising back up on her hands.

"Doesn't it occur to you," I said, "that they – whoever they are – might be after *you*, and they're only doing this to get me out of the way?"

"Why me?"

"Why Eddie Moon?" I asked. "Why Gus Marner? Bassett told me he thinks The Man – "

"Pecker-whistle?"

"If you say so....*Pecker-Whistle* wants to control the casinos in our region. It makes sense, in a way. You amortize your costs, make the whole industry crooked and reporting to the same people, and once you've established your control, you expand from there. One of the good things about law-breakers is that they don't like to play by rules, which is why we call them law-breakers. That usually keeps them from playing nice with each other. But if they do get organized, then the threat's bigger. We're in for a tough time if they control all gambling, drinking, and worse."

Elmira's hands slid off the foot of the bed and she almost tumbled off. It took her a minute to prop herself up again.

"Worse? What do you mean?"

"Opium, I think. I talked with Carmody about what he saw and he said he'd bet there was opium in the only bar he got close to. Miller said that stuff like opium is catching on. Lots of people take laudanum, and Miller sells it in his store, but he hears from other druggists that there are new ways to take poppy stuff through a needle. Once people start getting it that way, they can't stop."

"You think that's what they're after?" Elmira said.

"It's as good an answer as I can come up with. Get people to take something they *have* to have more of. Sell as much as you can and keep raising the prices. Get people to gamble and lose money in crooked games. Lend them money, charge them crazy interest. Sounds like a dream for the modern, organized criminal. Maybe criminals are setting up organizations, like the industrialists back East are setting up factories."

Elmira leaned forward and pinned my shoulders again. I couldn't tell if she was kidding or serious, angry or playful.

"We're no angels," she said. "What makes us better?"

"We draw lines," I said.

"Do we? What is so evil that we wouldn't do it?"

There's an odd belief among fighters, based on absolutely no fact at all of which I am aware, that you have to steer clear of women before a fight.

They steal your wind and the power of your punch, the tale goes.

Elmira was in a strange mood.

Was this her way of cheering me up? Or saying goodbye to the Josiah Hawke she knew before I got the part of the brain that made me Josiah Hawke hopelessly scrambled?

I asked myself these questions, along with whether what I wanted to do at this moment was worth the risk of losing my wind and my punch.

I was probably going to get slaughtered anyway.

So what the hell.

Chapter 60

I've always wondered where fight crowds appear from.

Start a fight, even in the middle of nowhere, and the gawkers materialize. Maybe they are the souls of evil-doers who'd sinned in past lives by fighting, and are condemned for eternity to appear at the first prospect of a fist being thrown.

I could find no other explanation for the sea of people who were on hand at 3:55 on a brilliantly sunny and unexpectedly warm Monday afternoon in the little corner of nowhere called Shadow Valley.

I kissed Elmira goodbye and waded through a churning mass of people on Front Street – men, women, children, people taking bets, people selling peanuts, and at least two men picking pockets, though I couldn't do anything about that now.

Dozens of people clapped me on the back as I made my way to the ring. They actually hit so hard my shoulder blades were starting to hurt, so I moved along at a trot.

Time moves pretty quickly, too, when you are caught up in events like a big fight. The introductions and instructions blurred by me like a downhill train and it seemed like just a few seconds before I had my shirt off and the lean, cat-quick John Stokes was flicking left jabs at me.

Chapter 61

Stokes was testing me out. I let a few go high over my head and I punched back high over his head, not with the intent of hitting him but getting my range and seeing how he'd react.

Stokes circled to his right. I could hear his feet scraping the hard soil in spite of all the crowd noise. Maybe it's the way sound travels when you're up against a hill, or maybe my mind just shut everything irrelevant out, but I could hear the pattern plainly: step-slide-step.

There was no wasted motion in the man. He didn't make circular windmills with his fists the way Ivey did, nor did he smile or taunt me. Instead, he simply found his range, tested my reactions, and then knocked me flat on my back.

***

It was a three-punch combination. The left came in fast but not too hard, but the right snuck in from low.

The right damn near put me out. But as sometimes happens – I don't know how, but take my word for it, it happens – you can virtually knock somebody out with one punch and wake him up with a follow-up.

When Stokes' left hook swept across my chin it jerked my head around and brought me awake like a splash of water.

But I still couldn't keep from falling.

The only sound I could hear as I lay on the ground was a long, collective groan. Not so much for my fate, I surmised, but from disappointment that the mob wouldn't have more time to enjoy my dismemberment.

Then I heard some high-pitched cursing and a slap, and my eyes focused enough to see that Swingle had thrown his hat on the ground in a rage. Then he stomped on it.

I took the full 30 seconds to rest. I didn't feel badly hurt but I was still dusting the cobwebs out and it wouldn't hurt for Stokes to believe I was in trouble.

When Carmody announced five seconds – he'd obtained a watch with a real second hand this time – I toed the scratch and then backed off immediately, popping jabs to keep Stokes at a distance. We were almost exactly the same height but my arms were a little longer and I can throw that jab all day. It gave him something to think about.

And I could *see* what he was thinking. He was thinking that if he threw that same combination it would finish me off.

The left flicked out. He was so fast I didn't have time to watch for the right. I just assumed he'd follow with that sneaky right from down low, so I ate the jab and whipped a left hook toward where I assumed his right fist would *not* be in a second – his fist would be low, coming up and targeted on me, and *not* in front of his face.

I guessed right. My hook slammed against his cheekbone and I fired the right straight down the middle and caught him flush in the face and Stokes went straight back and landed flat in the dirt, hitting with a slapping noise and raising a cloud of dust.

There was a delayed reaction from the crowd. Then they all screamed together, the noise arriving as suddenly as if it came from a faucet that had just been ratcheted open.

Stokes wasn't hurt. He scrambled up like an agile young dog and charged me. He was embarrassed to be put down by a nobody from nowhere.

He was in a blind rage.

He wanted to put his head in my chest and then bring his head up and clip me under the chin. I thought about kicking or kneeing him as he came in but I knew he'd be too fast for that, so I took a step back and lowered my head, too. We grappled for a second and I slipped sideways and pulled him forward.

He made the mistake of trying to push me away with his arm and I was able to wrap my arm around his and bend his arm back in a hammer lock.

I knew I couldn't hold him like that forever, so I sunk three shots into his kidneys before he twisted to face me and kicked me in the stomach.

The kick didn't land with much impact but had enough force to push me back.

Stokes stopped for a second, and took a few deep breaths.

So did I.

Then he brought his hands up again and moved toward me, circling. But a little more carefully this time. And he had murder in his eyes.

Chapter 62

After about twenty minutes, the crowd began to boo.

I couldn't blame them. It wasn't that neither of us wanted to fight. Rather, neither was willing to concede any advantage. I wasn't about to mix it up with a man whose hands struck like rattlesnakes, and Stokes wanted no part of wrestling with me. I'd jab and keep him away. He'd dart in with combinations that either missed or I was able to roll with, and I'd pepper him with the left jab to keep him, literally, at arm's length.

A few drifters began to question our manhood and some peanuts flew into the ring.

I responded to the hecklers with suggestions that they do something to themselves that as far as I can tell is anatomically impossible, and that set them into a frenzy of insults and insinuations.

I was grateful for every second of it. The slurs and the peanuts were hitting Stokes as well as me, but for him, they *hurt*.

Stokes was the champ, the prohibitive favorite, the guy with something to prove. I was just the sucker along for the ride. The presumptive loser with, therefore, nothing to lose.

Stokes got angrier as the match progressed and the shadows lengthened and the crowd turned crankier.

And then, suddenly, he was all over me like a swarm of bees.

***

He threw a sizzling left that snapped my head back and then came in low and hard, sinking both fists into my ribs. Getting hit there makes it hard to breathe, and I was gasping as I tried to spin away, keeping my elbows pinned against my side.

Stokes was setting me up, of course, and he knew it, and I knew it. The question was whether I could do anything about it.

When my hands were sufficiently low, Stokes threw a hook to my head, putting everything behind it. The blow caught me above the ear, and while I was able to turn with it, the force stunned me and I stumbled three steps to the right and caught myself with an outstretched hand before I fell.

Whether that position – holding myself off the ground with a hand – counted as being "down" was one of those complexities we had not anticipated. Carmody had never mentioned it in the instructions and Stokes apparently wasn't too concerned with the niceties because he aimed a kick at my ribs and connected, but not before I'd flung myself toward him, getting close enough to take some of the sting out of the kick and to use my arm to pin his ankle against my side.

I rolled toward him and dragged his leg beneath me and he went backward, holding himself off the ground with one hand.

Carmody, not the most energetic of referees, was leaning against the ropes with his arms crossed.

I looked at him for a second, and I think he shrugged.

If having a hand down didn't count for me, it didn't count for Stokes, either, so I so I backhanded him across the mouth.

Then he was down for sure, down flat on his back, the first blood of the fight smeared on his chin and the back of my hand, and Carmody pulled out his watch.

Chapter 63

Stokes was shaky when he got up, but a hurt man is often more dangerous that a fresh one. Stokes was in familiar territory.

He'd been a visitor in this strange haunted land before, and so had I.

It's a dream world where everything slows down, where the loudest sound is the rasp of your own breathing, and the pain you feel is real but somehow belongs to somebody else.

Stokes kicked at me but I checked it with the side of my foot, and he pivoted like a ballet dancer and kicked with the other foot, catching me behind the knee. I went down but didn't wait for the scratch because I sensed Stokes was more tired than I was and as tempting as my rest period was, it would work against me.

I danced in and caught him with my first real combination of the fight: a left jab, right cross, left hook, and then a right to his short ribs.

Stokes took a knee and scratched and then came after me like nothing had happened. He landed more of those sneaky-low rights, and then grabbed me by the hair and pulled me toward him.

Hair-pulling wasn't addressed in the rules, either.

With my head down, he was able to catch me with a knee to the forehead. I grabbed his leg and bulled forward but he was able to pull back. I sensed, somehow, that his hands were poised to come down on the back of my neck, and they did.

***

I looked at the dirt between my hands.

Somewhere in the dream world Carmody was yelling what sounded like *tin sickins*.

Then I heard what sounded like *kin ya make it ta scratch?*

Pain radiated the full length of my spine, and I had trouble looking up.

I knew I was supposed to get up but I wasn't sure why.

Then Carmody's face floated into view and he was asking me if I wanted to continue and I nodded, and nodding hurt like hell.

Then Stokes was on me again.

I threw the left for another five minutes while I circled and kept Stokes at bay.

"You can't keep this up all night," Stokes said.

It occurred to me that those were the first words I'd heard him say all night.

"Yes, I can," I said.

Chapter 64

But I couldn't.

My left arm was starting to go limp, and throwing my jab began to feel like I was slinging a piece of meat at his face.

Stokes got inside on me and we clenched and turned in a circle a few times. His head was under my chin and he kept butting upward, so I got a strange circular view of the sky as we pirouetted with my eyes forced skyward. There was a setting sun on one side and a rising moon on another. It was the brightest sun and moon I'd ever seen.

Everything, in fact, was painfully brilliant.

I saw brilliant flashes whenever Stokes landed.

I don't know what he was seeing, but he was breathing like a lathered horse. I figured if I could hold on, somehow, he might just exhaust himself from hitting me.

For what could have been five minutes or five hours, I flung my dead-meat left at him, and the boos started again. I looked over and saw that the crowd had thinned and somebody on the hill was actually asleep on the bench.

There was no sound now other than my breathing and the scratching of Stokes' feet in the dust as he kept up that clockwork pattern of circling and darting.

I tried a wide right and Stokes raised his arm and my fist caught his elbow.

And my right hand made that God-awful crunching sound again.

Stokes heard it.

I could tell he wanted to look at my hand but he kept his eyes fixed right on the center of my chest, where they are supposed to be.

If you look at the center of the chest, you can see where a man is intending to move. All the foot-work or flashy hand motion can't hide which way you're truly moving if you keep an eye on the breastbone.

Stokes could see me moving, all right.

But he couldn't see me thinking.

Chapter 65

I kept my right hand at my side.

Despite the crackling noise, the worst it ever emitted, the hand didn't hurt.

In fact, it was the only part of me that didn't hurt.

But Stokes didn't know that.

He circled to my right, my power side, which normally was the last place he'd want to be. I peppered him with jabs as best I could with my numb side-of-beef left arm, and ate some of his lefts that went over my right hand, which I didn't raise much beyond chest height.

Stokes was pressing me and I couldn't hold him off with the jab much longer.

I could physically not beat the younger, stronger man.

Not physically.

Stokes was still circling to the right, digging hooks into my side and unconcerned with my right hand.

He cracked me in the ribs again, still oblivious to my right hand.

Until I put the last bit of strength I possessed behind my right hand and drove it into his mouth.

Stokes stepped back, wobbled.

I was wary of him playing possum so I took my time moving in and tried a left hook, which connected, and then brought the right across, smartly, and snapped his head to the left.

And then I hooked him with the left. The arm had temporarily come back to life. I snapped his head to the right.

His eyes went vacant.

And then I hit him again. Left. Right. Left. Right.

He seemed to be made of iron.

"Go *down,* you son of a bitch," I said.

And then I snapped his head back and forth twice again, and he stood with his arms to his side, staring directly into the blinding, slanting sun that was dipping below the trees, and I reared back, taking my time, and crushed an overhand right to his jaw.

He pitched forward.

When they fall on their faces, that generally means they're not going to get up anytime soon.

And then Carmody raised my hand and then he picked me up and spun me like a madman dancing with a scarecrow, damn near breaking my ribs and getting me so dizzy I was afraid I was going to throw up.

As he whirled me, I saw that crazy moon, the red sliver of sun, and the mortified face of Bassett. I saw it over and over, round and round, until I told Carmody he was going to finish the job Stokes started and begged him to stop. Or at least spin me the other way for a while.

Carmody set me down gently as a vase.

"Get the money," I said.

As banged-up as I was, it occurred to me that there were dozens of people here we didn't know, most of them armed, and they might take exception to paying off a huge bet they did not expect to lose.

As soon as the world stopped spinning, I saw that Bassett had gone white. Literally. He was the color of fresh snow and he was visibly trembling. He looked around like he was going to make a break for it but he was hemmed in by the crowd and couldn't move.

Carmody didn't bother with small talk. He just reached over the top rope, stuck his hand inside Bassett's coat, searched around a bit, and snatched the wad. He also was appropriating Stokes' $500 loser's share, but I figured they would know where to find me if they wanted to claim it.

"Let's get to the Spoon," Carmody said. "Quick."

I climbed through the ropes and pushed through the crowd.

Everybody wanted to talk, stepping in front of me, grabbing me, hugging me, slapping me on the back.

Carmody insistently prodded me forward.

Carmody, as he is apt to remind me from time to time, is no dummy. He'd apparently instructed Oak, Miller, Swingle, Bosco, and Taza to bring their rifles and form a wedge as soon as the fight ended and escort me back to the Spoon.

I took that as a compliment because it meant that Carmody anticipated the possibility I'd still be able to walk, and possibly might be in possession of quite a bit of money. I savored that thought as much as the memory of Stokes kissing the dirt on Front Street.

Carmody hustled me through the batwings, and instructed Oak, who drew up the rear, to keep everybody out and shut the inside locking door.

"We'll be serving in a few minutes," Carmody shouted before Oak slammed it shut.

Carmody told us all it was going to be a long night and we'd best be on our guard, and then he said he'd go fetch Elmira, wherever she was, and tell her the good news.

"Poor girl's probably hiding under the bed," Carmody said.

Everybody laughed except Miller.

Miller was holding a note that he'd picked up off the bar.

"They've kidnapped Elmira," he said.

Chapter 66

"You have caused us time and trouble," Miller read aloud, moving the paper toward the window. No one had lit the lanterns yet, and the sun had set, but the moonlight was so intense I could see it beaming through the pane and illuminating the dancing dust particles we'd raised.

"We have your pretty little girlfriend. If you want her released unharmed, meet us tonight at a location that will be provided to you. Ride alone and unarmed to the summit of White Rocks. There is a lightning-struck tree at the very top and you will find further directions leading you to the girl written on a paper nailed to the tree. It is mostly open land and we have sentries and we will be able to see if you have been followed. Do not think about playing tricks. If you come we will let her go unharmed."

I guess I should have exhibited some wailing and gnashing of teeth, but I hadn't had time to turn back into a civilized person yet. I was still in fight mode.

And this was the next round.

"What's the rest of it say?" I said.

Miller read on with some reluctance. I could surmise there was more writing that he'd read because the moonlight showed right through the thin paper, and I could see the backside of an odd, old-fashioned style of handwriting. Or maybe it just appeared strange because of the angle.

"If you do not come, we will release her anyway," Miller said. "We will send her back to you one piece at a time."

"*Bassett*," I said. "He's the only one besides us that knew Elmira was staying here alone. I told him."

Carmody was already moving toward the door and he was gone by the time my sentence ended.

"Carmody will get him and bring him back," I said to no one in particular. "From now until this ends, we have to be like Carmody. Think ahead, act fast."

And then my motivational speech ended when I got dizzy and sunk to the floor.

Chapter 67

Taza brought me back by splashing me with some greasy dishwater we kept behind the bar.

I hadn't gone completely out, just faded into a gray place.

"You in any shape to do this?" Oak asked.

"No," I said. "But it's not like I have a choice."

"You need beer," Taza said, moving behind the bar.

"This isn't the time," I said.

"You drink something," Taza said, handing me the mug in a way that made it clear he would pour it down my throat if I didn't comply. "You faint like little girl because you sweat so much and have no food or drink since before fight."

Swingle felt it necessary to add some commentary.

"He went on his face because he just had his punkin bashed for two hours."

"That, too," Taza said.

And then Bosco began talking in that same resonant baritone that carried to the balconies of

Europe, but this time the voice was different. My head was too foggy for me to put a finger on it.

"Taza is right," Bosco said. "You need some liquid and some sugar and beer's the best we can do right now. You have to be able to get to that tree. We're going to track you without them knowing and before they kill you, we're going to kill *them*. All of them."

I was about to ask him how when the tumbler on the front lock-door turned and Bassett was propelled in like some dynamite blew him into the room.

Chapter 68

"Caught him trying to high-tail on the delta trail," Carmody said. "The crowd slowed him down."

Bassett had landed on his hands and knees after Carmody pushed him and he scuttled to his feet.

Miller touched Carmody on the shoulder and handed him the letter.

And then Swingle drew his revolver and jammed the barrel into Bassett's crotch.

"We ain't got time to screw around roughing you up," Swingle said. "Where's the boss lady?"

"I don't know," Bassett said. "I swear to God. I didn't even know they'd taken her until Carmody told me."

"But you tipped them off," I said.

Bassett looked at me with an expression that betrayed the last emotion I would have expected from him.

He was angry.

"They took my *daughter*," he said, spitting the words. "They said they'd hurt her if I didn't spy on you and report back what I heard. They got interested when I told them Elmira would be waiting the fight out here. I didn't know what they was doing then, and I don't know where they took her now."

"The first shot blows your balls off," Swingle said. "I'll let you feel it for a minute and then I'll ask the question again and if I still don't get no answer I'll put the next one in your head. Where is Elmira?"

Bassett shut his eyes.

"I don't know," he said.

Bassett opened his eyes and looked at me.

"I told you I wasn't your friend. That was the best I could do for you."

I believed him.

I wobbled over to Swingle and put a hand on his bony shoulder.

"I think he's telling the truth. Let's keep him alive for later. Maybe he knows something that none of us knows is important now."

"Can't I just shoot his balls off?"

"Not a good idea," I said. "He might die anyway."

"One ball?"

"Maybe later. We need to keep him alive."

'Want me to lock him in my cell?"

"No time for that," I said, and drove my right hand into Bassett's jaw. My fist made that damn crackling noise again, but it still worked fine.

Chapter 69

"We have to get started right now," Bosco said, his baritone roaring, seemingly from the bowels of the earth. "So everybody *get your heads outta yer asses and shuddup.*"

I felt the urge to reach over and push Carmody's jaw up because it had dropped to his chest.

I'd never been to New Jersey, and as far as I knew Carmody hadn't either, but now we knew how the natives talked.

"He's been beat to shit." Bosco said, "and he's exhausted, so we've got to do most of this ourselves. We have to follow him and not be seen. Carmody is the best tracker here, maybe the best tracker anywhere, but they'll be watching and we know the path to Elmira is through open land, so even Carmody will have trouble staying out of sight."

"So what do we do?" Miller said.

Bosco looked out the window.

"Do you think it's going to stay bright like this for a while?" he asked of no one in particular.

"Yes, all night," Carmody said. "There ain't a cloud in the sky and this is the hunter's moon."

Bosco tilted his head.

"Two brightest moons of the year is the harvest moon and the hunter's moon," Carmody said, holding up that damned finger. There's never a situation too urgent to preclude him delivering a lecture.

"Harvest moon's the second to last full moon in October, lets the farmers work all night. Right now's the last full moon in October, the night you hunt and stock up for the winter."

"How's that help us?" Oak said. "Doesn't it make it worse? They can see us coming."

"And anyway," Swingle said, "who put you in charge?"

Miller held up a palm.

"Let him speak."

Bosco nodded and moved toward the bar.

"Everybody in this room except me has combat experience, and Carmody and Taza are both expert trackers and woodsmen."

"I am better," Taza said.

"The point is," Bosco said, "I don't know much about that either, but – "

"The hell you is," Carmody said.

"BUT," Bosco boomed, and I could actually feel his voice buzz in my chest, "tonight will be won or lost on deception and trickery, and that's what I do."

Bosco went behind the bar and hefted the canvas I'd spread to catch the paint splatters from when I painted the mirror, a job I still hadn't finished and, the way things were going, might never finish. The top frame was a smooth brown but the bottom was still the color of dead mice.

"Do you have more of this cloth?" Bosco said.

"Enough to rig a sailboat," Carmody said.

Bosco held up the paint can and raised an eyebrow.

"How about this?"

"Enough to paint the damn sailboat, but why?"

Bosco thought for a second and then picked up a mug and smashed the mirror.

Chapter 70

I knew the way to White Rocks and while I'd never been to the summit I figured the trail would lead me there.

I was wearing a white shirt that Oak had lent me. It was too big but that was all right, because maybe whoever was watching me would miss the knife that Carmody had rigged between my shoulder blades.

We'd determined there was no point in my trying to hide a gun because they'd search me and undoubtedly pat my pockets, and probably pat down those places tough guys aren't supposed to pat on another man. But they might not think to check the upper back.

Besides, if my hands were raised, I'd be in a good position to reach the knife. Carmody said it was a throwing knife, and I told him that since I'd never thrown a knife it wouldn't do me much good, but he assured me that it was plenty good for stabbing, too.

The white shirt was bright under the moonlight, and I'd worn my Boss of the Plains hat, which was a light tan. Elmira had bought it for me, spent a lot of money on it, and had asked Carmody to retrieve it from some deep woods after it had been shot off my head in an ambush a year ago.

The hat had a wide band. In the back of the hat, Bosco had stuck two shards from the smashed mirror.

The light from the hunter's moon bathed the trail in a strange silvery glow that seemed blissfully peaceful. I was mesmerized by the beauty.

It would be a nice night to die, I thought.

They might gun me down if they figured out the mirror trick, but for the most part I assumed they would be watching me *coming*, not going. And once I was past whoever was watching, I wasn't sure if they'd retain much interest because they'd be interested in seeing whether I was followed, not following me.

But from the back, under the hunter's moon, if you knew what you were looking for, the glint of light reflecting from the rear, you could probably see me for a mile.

Chapter 71

The lightning-struck tree was at the very tip of the mountain, and it cast a bizarre angular shadow in the moonlight.

I was dizzy when I dismounted, and had to lean against my mount's shoulder for a second before reading the note.

I was not exactly on top of the Rocky Mountains, but White Rocks had a summit nonetheless. It was a respectable small mountain or a large hill. I've never known what the difference is, but it didn't matter at the moment.

All I knew was that when I looked around it was stunningly beautiful.

I'd only been here for a couple years but I knew the geography pretty well.

Carmody will tell you that I can't find my ass with both hands and a telescope but I'm good with maps – I was a tactical officer, among other assignments, during the war – and I've spent a lot of time in this part of the Hill Country. I could see the vast quilt of cultivated fields, awash with the moonlight that was at once buttery and silvery, like Elmira's hair. I knew which field belonged to which rancher or farmer.

I could see the lights on the stable, the highest building in Shadow Valley. Bosco had snatched up every lantern he could find and lit the hayloft up.

Carmody will also tell you that I'm blind as a mole, but while I don't have his superhuman eyesight I see as well as any man and better than most, and I could make out the glowing rectangular shape of the big window of the loft, probably a mile away.

The window where Carmody would be waiting, watching through his bronze spyglass.

From my perch on the summit, I also could see the entire river and creek system for miles, and I could even make out the glistening turbulence in the places where waterways joined and the rushing waters fought each other for dominance.

The waterways were laid out like a silvery map. The scene I was taking in looked exactly like a living, breathing, glowing version the map Carmody retrieved from the office before I left on my journey.

The map Bosco had told us to study and quickly list the most important thirty landmarks it showed.

***

The note told me to ride into the mouth of the small box canyon called Slate Hollow.

It was a perfect location to capture and kill me, I thought. It was isolated, but everybody knew where it was, so there was no chance I'd be stymied trying to find it. And I'd be coming in low, riding through land with no cover, and they would be waiting above me.

Watching me enter Slate Hollow.

I began to cough. I reached into the pocket of Oak's flowing white shirt and plucked out a handkerchief and retched into it.

Then I wiped my face and felt the sticky blood I knew was clinging around my nose.

I looked at the little smear on the handkerchief, as though I were surprised.

That's what I hoped the men watching me thought.

I knew they were watching me. I could *feel* it. After all these years in my business, you can feel the eyes.

I'm sure they could see me plainly, although probably not clearly enough to notice that I was reading the small, precise lettering Bosco had instructed Miller to ink on the handkerchief.

I actually remembered the number, though I double-checked it on the handkerchief.

Slate Hollow was landmark number 27.

I walked in back of the horse and doubled over with another coughing fit.

I coughed twice, violently, and each time I convulsed I twisted the mirror shard that I held in the handkerchief in the direction of the stable window.

Two coughs, two flashes.

Then I sniffed, balanced myself on the flank of the horse, but doubled over again.

This time I coughed exactly seven times.

Chapter 72

Even though Slate Hollow was only a mile away, I had to stop to rest several times. I also became confused twice, and had to double back to take the right fork.

But I was making slow, deliberate progress, as good as you could expect from a man who'd just been in a very long prizefight.

At least that's how I hoped the eyes in the woods would see it.

When I arrived at the mouth of the canyon, I hitched the Steeldust to a tree – the last tree before the opening – and walked the rest of the way in with my hands up.

I was limping. It seemed like it took forever before I was close enough for them to grab me.

Chapter 73

The Man's face was frozen with a cold hatred that emanated from within him.

He didn't change expressions as he beat me.

I was able to roll with most of the punches, and he swung wide and wild, sometimes hitting my shoulders or the shoulders of the men who were holding me by the arms.

But I could feel the blows adding up and my vision was constricting, like I was looking down a gray, sparkly tunnel.

Elmira was on the ground, lying on her side, tied hand and foot, and of course he was making her watch.

There were more than a dozen of them. Some looked like pugs, with flat noses and puffy ears. Others had the fancy leather rigs and the bored, slouchy look of gunfighters.

The Man was breathing heavily now. Wheezing. He'd punched himself out.

He looked at me with that same icy ferocity.

I looked back. I realized that I knew him. I *didn't* know him, but I *knew* him, somehow.

He reached under his coat and drew out a gleaming nickel pocket pistol.

"Why are you doing this?" I asked.

The question caught him by surprise. Men about to be murdered usually don't strike up conversations.

But I had a feeling he had something to say, and the longer I could keep him talking, the better.

He hit me on the temple with the barrel of his pocket pistol. The men holding me flinched. They knew enough about guns to know that they can go off when used as a club.

The Man probably knew that, too, but he didn't care.

"You have caused me many problems," he said, slowly and formally, in a voice sprinkled with the paprika of an accent I could not identify.

"Then why didn't you just kill me to begin with?"

He hit me again.

"Because you have friends. Your type always has friends. The idiots who will come looking for anyone who hurts their idiot type, just because the idiot wears a star."

My badge is actually in the shape of a shield, not a star, but I didn't think that detail would hold his attention, so I asked him who he was.

And he hit me again and told me it was none of my business.

"I saw your name on an envelope," I said. "Weird name. Longer than the damned envelope. Something like *putz-a-weasel.*"

He was angry now. His hand shook as he clubbed me again.

"Or *pecker-whistle.*"

"You filthy rube jackass," he said. "Call me by my proper name."

He backhanded me with the barrel this time and told me to address him as what sounded to me like *GREG-or Pruzh-teh-ZELL.*

The realization hit a second before the gun barrel hit me again.

The face was the same. Just subtract the mustache, take away four inches, and add twenty years, and you had the man who was beating me.

"Say it," he barked before he raked the barrel backhand across my forehead. "Say my name."

I was starting to lose consciousness. And I was bleeding from where the tip of the barrel had sliced my head and it was hard to see even with the crazy moonlight.

"He didn't like the clunky name, did he?" I yelled, surprised to hear my voice echo back at me. "Always having to explain it and spell it when he tried to sell his services as a murderer."

I could still see enough to notice that the word got his attention.

"Murderer," I yelled, and then I yelled it again, and again, hearing it collide with the echo and fight for attention with it.

"You are the murderer," he hissed.

"So instead of your unpronounceable name, he called himself Purcell. And he tried to kill me, and you probably set him up to do it so you could squeeze your way in on that railroad deal."

The Man said nothing and bared his teeth and I knew I was right.

"He was pretty good," I said. "But I was better."

He screamed through clenched teeth and drew back the gun again.

The men holding me tightened their grip on the back of my arms.

And then a cricket chirped.

Finally.

Chapter 74

Carmody didn't want to use any of his collection of bird calls as a signal, because there aren't that many birds going about their business in the middle of the night. So we decided that a cricket would be less obtrusive.

Just to make sure that I don't mix him up with any real wildlife, Carmody made the sound twice, paused, and then once, the way no normal creature of the wild would dream of doing it.

After the third chirp, I jerked forward toward The Man and screamed.

No one in their right mind runs *toward* a man with a gun, and that's what the goons holding me were thinking, because they weren't prepared for it. They were expecting me to run backward. So I broke free and batted The Man's gun aside but I couldn't grab it.

He kept hold of the gun and skittered back three steps.

It took me a second to dig out the knife because it got tangled in Oak's shirt but then I had it and launched it at him. It gleamed in the moonlight.

To my surprise it hit him, point-first, in the shoulder. Not enough to do any real damage, but it stuck. And it gave me the distraction I needed.

I knocked the gun aside just as it went off. I could feel the bullet crease my skull.

The impact was harder than anything Stokes had landed. I figured my brains weren't blown out, though, because I was still functioning, but I didn't know how long I could stay conscious.

And I didn't particularly care.

All I cared about was squeezing the throat between my hands.

***

There was blood in my eyes and I could only see vague crimson shapes and outlines of movement.

It was dream-like, but even as the moonlight grew dim I knew what happened next wasn't a dream. A mound of dirt from which small branches sprouted somehow stood up and opened fire. Then there was an Apache war-whoop and more gunfire.

I let go of the throat between my hands and pitched forward toward Elmira. It was less of a run and more of a controlled fall, my legs moving just fast enough to keep from pitching forward, until I wanted to pitch forward, until I was sprawled over top of her to shield her from the bullets.

And then there was more blasting, the smell of gunpowder, the taste of blood, and a deep and strangely peaceful sleep that lasted, I was told, for almost three days.

Chapter 75

"**D**on't worry," Elmira's voice said from somewhere off to my side. "You're not blind. We just had to cover your eyes with the bandage."

There was a rustling sound.

"Here," I heard her say as she pulled some gauzy stuff aside and brilliant, merciless light assaulted me. "You can see Tom in front of you."

I saw Carmody's face looming over me, not more than two feet from mine, filling my field of vision.

"Please," I said. "Put the bandage back."

"Ingrate," Carmody said.

My voice was creaky and Elmira held a glass to my lips and managed to spill all of it on me but I didn't care.

"Are you all right?" I said.

"Who are you asking?" Elmira said.

"Does it matter?" I said, annoyed, and then the pain hit me and I could see the futility in getting drawn into the debate.

"I'm asking anybody and everybody in general."

"I'm fine," Elmira said. "You did crank my neck some when you heaved yourself on top of me but it'll clear up."

"None of us was hurt much," Carmody said. "Taza caught a bullet in the shoulder, but you know how he is. Bragged about it for a day and then took it out hisself with a knife, right at the bar."

"I almost threw up," Elmira said.

"Swingle was grazed," Carmody said. "So was Bosco. Nothing much."

"How about the goons?"

"Six dead," Camody said. "The rest surrendered. Damn near dislocated their joints putting their hands up after the first volley."

"There's something I have to know," I said. "Did you really dress up as a pile of dirt?"

Carmody's voice got that peevish old-man timbre he affects when he's irritated. In twenty years he'll probably sound like that all the time.

"Now, you make it sound crazy," he said. "But Bosco was right on the mark. He said that they'd choose a place where the approach didn't have much cover, and he was right. So he covered a tarp with splashes of brown paint and stuck some branches on it. Bosco and me, we'd advance a little, hunker down, and creep up again. Taza and Swingle did the same from the other side. Oak and Miller ain't so good at creeping so they stayed back and charged when we started firing."

Elmira spoke up.

"It was awful watching you get pistol-whipped. But Tom said you did the right thing, egging him on and all. It was a good distraction so they could creep up and get in position. They couldn't just open fire because they were afraid you and I would be hit."

I could hear her start to sniffle.

"Tom said he knew you'd make a distraction and then you'd shield me. And you *did.*"

Then she let loose with the wailing for a while.

"*Putz-a-Weasel* is alive," she said as soon as she caught her breath. "You almost broke his neck and he couldn't talk for a while, but he's in jail now and got his voice back and he's dancing.

"Dancing?"

"She means 'singing,'" Carmody said. "Elmira never did pick up outlaw slang. He's in a state prison and facing about a million years if he don't fess up to some stuff, so he's making like a songbird."

Something didn't add up. I had to see their faces to make sense of it.

I reached up and tugged at the bandage.

"If I pull this up, will my brains fall out?"

"Your skull is fine," Elmira said. "Exceptional, in fact."

Carmody explained.

"Your head bone is incredible thick, according to the doctor. Which came as a surprise to no one here. You just got a bad cut and a little crease in the side of your noggin bone. But that graze to the head was hell of an impact, and that, on top of the beatings you took all night, put you out for quite a spell."

I pulled the bandages up and squinted through eyes as narrow as I could keep them and still see anything. It appeared to be late afternoon and there was some dim amber light cutting in through the window. To me, the room blazed like noon in the desert.

I covered my eyes again.

Then the realization hit me as hard as the light.

"*State prison*? How'd that come about?"

"I can't see who you're looking at," Elmira said. "Are you asking me or –"

"We did what we probably should have done in the first place," Carmody said. "I rode up to Austin and told the whole story to your friend Harbold. He had his Ranger buddies and some constables all over it. He told me to tell you that you should've talked with him earlier."

"Maybe *we* should have," I said, hoping Carmody picked up on the plural, "but like we talked about before – what would we have told him? All we had were a bunch of disconnected threads."

I had adjusted the bandages so I was looking through one layer of gauze and I could see Carmody nod.

"You're right," Carmody said. "We had a lot of stuff going on but nothing to tie it all together. If I was in his place, I just would have wrote it off to co-incidence. But when we had half a dozen dead bodies and the information from…what's his name?

"*Putz-a-weasel*," I said.

"I think it's *Prick-da-whistle*," Elmira corrected.

"The information from Purcell's father," Carmody said, "tied it all together. And while you was napping, we got busy. We tracked down most of this stuff. I went to Austin and found that guy Ludd. Purcell's father fingered Ludd as the guy who started our particular problems in the first place. Ludd planted the marked cards with the wholesaler and sent in the sharpie who Swingle shot. And beat up the wholesaler so we'd be forced to pay more for supplies from Old Man Purcell's associates. And we was able to put together the same patterns in all the towns they'd wormed their way into. And anybody who stood up to them, like Moon and Marner, got their brains blowed out and Ludd's men set it up as a suicide."

Elmira sat next to me on the bed, lifted the gauze, and ran a cloth over my eyes.

"Purcell's father admitted that he was behind everything," she said, "starting with the murder of Billy Gannon. His son was the front man, but the father pulled the strings."

I sat up a little and it hurt but I felt a little better and took a drink and got most of it in my mouth this time.

"So all this was just to get back at me?"

"Not all of it," Carmody said. "The old man wanted to take over the territory. But if you got killed or crippled in the process, that was gravy. When they couldn't get rid of you, they took Elmira to lure you to a place where you could both be made to disappear. More risk than they wanted to take, but they figured that if they was sure you wasn't followed they could dispose of the bodies where they would never be found...no bodies, no crime, no link, no case. And *both* of you would be out of the way. More gravy."

"Gravy," I said, and lay back down. It was cold and damp where Elmira had dumped the first glass of water but it felt bracing.

It let me know I was alive.

"You'd better get some more sleep," Elmira said.

"Wait a minute," I said, and this time I was able to sit upright. "This just doesn't make any sense. The old man is rich and smart and can probably afford to bribe everybody in Texas and hire an army of lawyers. You're telling me that he caved in and confessed to everything the minute they threw him in a state cell?"

Elmira and Carmody exchanged glances, shifted their feet a little, exchanged glances again, and then Carmody shrugged and cleared his throat.

"He did some talking before the state got involved," Carmody said. "A *lot* of talking."

"While he was in Swingle's room," Elmira said. "Swingle's *cell,* I mean."

"Swingle got a little peeved at being put out of his living quarters," Carmody said, "and he wasn't too happy about getting shot, neither. Them graze wounds sting like crazy."

Elmira smiled, reached over and patted my knee.

"But Swingle volunteered to spend the rest of the night watching the prisoner and they had all night to talk," she said.

"All night," Carmody said, shaking his head, giving a far-away look.

"All night," Elmira said, and hugged herself as though she were suddenly cold.

"You best not concern yourself with the details," Carmody said as they both hurried out the door.

Chapter 76

I wobbled on down to the Spoon a couple of times over the next week and felt good enough to play piano on the last day of the month, which was also All Hallowe'en, which would put folks in a festive mood. I hoped they didn't turn rowdy because for the time being there wasn't a damn thing I could do about it if they did.

I didn't know any appropriate music, so I just played what came to mind. My hand worked all right, even though it kept making that crackling noise. My brain seemed to be functioning. I remembered the notes and the names of the songs, although it sometimes took a while.

But then, it's never easy to remember a song you heard once or twice.

I tried some creepy parts of Beethoven, and that seemed to work, although I wasn't sure Hallowe'en meant spooky stuff to everybody. It's different things to people in different parts of the country, and some people who migrated here actually never heard of it.

When I was a boy, we called in Snap Apple Night, because we spent it bobbing for apples. We didn't dress up or beg for candy, though we had heard that kids elsewhere did just that and the idea made eminent sense to us at the time so we made it an instant tradition.

I understand that in some places All Hallowe'en is a big night for costume parties, but I had not observed any of that here. That's why I was surprised when Bosco came in.

I hadn't seen him since I came to. Carmody and Elmira told me he'd left town on business but would be back to see me as soon as I was up and around.

And here he was decked out as a town marshal.

And nicely, too. Unlike my dull gunmetal gray shield, his badge was pointed and fashioned of gleaming bronze with blue inlays.

I waved him over and stopped playing so I could shake hands and took a close look.

It was a hell of a badge. There was a circle inside the star with another circle emblazoned on it. Above the circle was a ribbon design stamped into the medal, with the words *City Marshal* stamped in blue.

Beneath the circle was another ribbon device with blue lettering.

It said, *New Paradise, Tex.*

"That's for real," I said.

"For real," he said. "I was around when the state boys cleaned up the infestation and they heard I was good with a gun. It was their idea. The town officials were fine with it. They never had a marshal. You don't know you need one until you need one."

"Sometimes it takes a jolt to get them to cough up the money," I said.

"They pay all right," Bosco said. "And they sprung for a deputy, too. That's how I happen to be here. Swingle is covering for me tonight."

I stopped playing.

"Swingle? He's your *deputy?*"

"Good man with a gun," Bosco said.

"A prodigy," I agreed. "A *genius.* But as far as temperament goes, he might need some supervision. From one marshal to another. But I don't mean to tell you your business, Bosco."

"Got you," Bosco said. "Thanks for all you've done. And from now on, let's make it Bill. Bill Guillaume."

He turned and beckoned and Gina and Louisa came over and said hello. They asked how I was feeling and I said I was on the mend and then they told me how they were looking forward to a new life that did not involve touring, wagons, and hotels.

They said they'd stop by later and I watched them walk away, though I paid particular attention to Gina and Louisa, who were both dressed in the same tight pants they were wearing when I first met them.

Then I heard Elmira said, "Excuse me. Sorry to interrupt."

I had no doubt what she meant.

"I guess they think they'll like sharing the life of a town marshal," she said.

I said they probably would welcome the change.

"The first time they lie awake all night wondering if their man is going to get over his latest beating, or his latest bullet, maybe they'll change their mind."

I was surprised by her tone and the way the conversation was headed.

It comes with the territory, I told her.

And then she made a remark about how some women are drawn to violent men and I felt a little heat rise in me.

"People are drawn to each other because of who they are," I said.

I smiled when I said the next part because I wanted to seem playful but I wanted to make a point, too.

"The night before the fight," I said, "you were scared but a little excited, too. Am I right?"

"Maybe a little," she said, giggling a little. The tension broke.

"Were *you* scared?" she asked.

"Yes."

"Were you excited?"

"Yes."

"Excited because of me or because of the fight?"

"Just you," I said.

She liked that and put her head on my shoulder.

Carmody appeared and set his drink on the top of the piano, which leaves rings in the wood, so Elmira plucked it off, wiped the surface with her sleeve, and suddenly downed it herself.

"It's been a couple of rough weeks," she said, and then began to cry.

Carmody and I both talked softly to her.

"Everything's fine now," Carmody said. "Better than it was before."

"He got hit in the head a thousand times," Elmira told him, speaking as if I weren't there.

Then she looked right at me.

"How much more of this do you think you can take?" she said. "How much more can *I* take?"

Carmody cut in.

"Let's just enjoy ourselves. Josiah's melon is fine. The doctor said he had a skull like a bull. And anyway, he weren't too smart to begin with."

"Guess you're right," Elmira said. She smiled a little and wiped her nose on her sleeve.

"Since you don't know no spooky stuff," Carmody said, "give us something a little cheerful. Do the Alabama Blossoms song again."

I nodded and cracked my knuckles, which made Elmira wince, and put my hands in position over the keys.

After a beat, Carmody asked me if I remembered it.

Of course I did, I told him, and I started to play.

It just took me a little longer than usual to remember how it started.

And then I felt the beer trickle down the back of my shirt.

I stopped playing and turned around and saw another beefy kid with a curled lip. This one had blond hair and carried a gun down low, the way people who like to be taken for gunslingers wear it.

"Sorry," he said, making clear that he wasn't. "Didn't do it on purpose. No sane man would spill beer on the heavyweight champion of the West."

"I suppose you're a fighter," I said.

"I suppose you're right," he said. "And I ain't never been beat. And I suppose you're too old to give me a shot. Old men scare easy, I been told."

"Kid," I said, "right now I'm so beat up I can barely bang on this piano."

"I can wait," he said. "But you're stalling."

"Do you see this hand?" I asked, and flexed it, and it made that noise again.

"So?" the kid said, confused. It didn't take much to confuse him.

"As beat up as it is, it's the one part of me that still works. It can get that gun out of my holster and pull the trigger and blow your brains out before you can finish reaching for yours."

He licked his lips and was thinking about his next move. Carmody took a step toward him and then the man reborn as Bill Guillaume walked over.

"I see you got your friends coming to your rescue," the kid said.

"I don't want to interfere," Guillaume said. "I just want to show you something."

And then Guillaume drew. The metal hissed on the leather and before the wide-eyed kid could blink the barrel of Guillaume's gun was pressed to his forehead.

"He did that to me," Guillaume said, "before I could get my gun out of my holster."

And then he pushed a little harder than he had to and the kid tottered a step back.

Guillaume reholstered.

"So you're welcome to try," he said. "I just wanted to let you know what you're in for."

Then Elmira told the kid to leave. Her voice was trembling.

He backed toward the door, looking as though he were going to bolt through it as soon as he said something that he clearly wanted to say.

"I come looking for a fair fight," the kid said, his voice quavering a little, "and you have your buddy run me out at gunpoint."

"What's your name?" I said. He didn't expect the question, and it startled him.

"Winsley," he said. "Sam Winsley."

"Sam," I said, "it's time for you to move along. There's nothing here that will turn out well for you."

"I want a chance at that title, and I want a chance at you. Not with guns, but with fists."

"No you don't."

"And why is that?" he said, backing out the door.

I saw that Elmira was looking at me, and she was crying again.

"Because I'm retired from fighting," I lied, and I turned back to the piano.

THE END

About the Author

Carl Dane is an award-winning, best-selling author of fiction and non-fiction. He has published 22 nonfiction books, four novels, a collection of short stories, and has had one play produced.

He was born in San Antonio, and has maintained a lifelong interest in the Old West and American history. He is a member of the Western Writers of America, the Sons of Union Veterans of the Civil War, and the Sons of the American Revolution.

Carl is a career journalist and a college professor, and lives in suburban New Jersey.

He often writes and lectures about ethical dilemmas. He has testified about ethical issues before Congress and has discussed related topics on a variety of national broadcast and cable news programs.

Reviewers have consistently praised Carl Dane's work for its inventive focus on questions of right and wrong, deft humor, crackling plot, and warm and believable characterizations.

Follow Carl at www.carldane.com

Made in the USA
Middletown, DE
12 December 2022

18200720R00184